THE
MASKED
WOMAN

THE MASKED WOMAN

JOHNSTON McCULLEY

WILDSIDE PRESS

THE MASKED WOMAN

"The Masked Woman" originally appeared in
The Washington Post, January 2, 1921.

Selected and edited by John Gregory Betancourt for the
Wildside Pulp Classics line. For more information, visit

THE MASKED WOMAN

I

A Sort of Rubicon

There it was again—that faint scraping sound so foreign to the neighborhood; a sound pregnant with possibilities, including mystery unfathomable, violence, tragedy, experience, the lure of the unknown. Prof. James Xenophon Salwick sat up straight in his chair and allowed his imagination to soar. Troubled with insomnia continually, Prof. Salwick knew all the nocturnal sounds of the locality, and this he recognized as utterly new.

He put on his spectacles, made sure that they rested lightly on the sore spot on his nose, and then arose and stretched out his arms. He was not a large man—perhaps five feet six inches tall—and his general appearance indicated brains rather than brawn. But, early in his college days, Prof. Xenophon Salwick had been assured by an elderly lecturer, who looked as if he had both feet in the grave up to the knees, that a brain worker could achieve great heights only but keeping his body in suitable condition—and Prof. Salwick had done just that.

"It is evident," he told himself, "that some misguided individual has invaded my poor apartment."

A moment he hesitated, and then he reached out and turned the knob of the door that opened into his living room. The door itself was opened an inch at a time, and cautiously until there was space enough for the professor to slip through. This he did, silently, his senses alert. He continued along the wall until he reached the light switch. And he snapped on the lights.

Brute Wilger whirled from the desk he had been investigating with the aid of an electric torch. He snarled like a rat at bay. He wore no mask, and the professor got an instant look at his face. It was a brutal face; the eyes were small and black and glittering, and set too close together, the ears extended from the head, and the head itself was shaped something like a bullet. Black hair adorned it, but the hair was closely cropped.

"Well," Brute Wilger snarled.

The professor cleared his throat.

"Will you be kind enough to sit down?"

"Youse'll be glad to sit down yourself, like a little man, and let me fix youse so I'll have a chance at a getaway!" Brute Wilger informed him. "And, if youse don't, I'll just naturally muss up this place with youse!"

"I assure you that violence is unnecessary," declared the professor. "I have not the slightest intention of handing you over to the police. I should like to have a conversation with you. I am greatly interested in anthropology."

Brute Wilger had continued to approach during the professor's recital. And now he sprang—swiftly, silently, his eyes glittering malevolently and his teeth set. His gnarled hands clutched at the professor's throat; his weight struck against the man of science.

Brute Wilger realized, when it was too late, that he had made a mistake. Stooped shoulders and spectacles and a knowledge of something more than low life did not indicate physical weakness, the Brute discovered. In some peculiar manner, Prof. James Xenophon Salwick accomplished a neat side-step. His hands flashed up and grasped Brute Wilger's wrists, and he gave a quick wrench.

Wilger uttered a cry of pain. As it left his lips, he found himself whirled around neatly and thrown to the floor. The professor did something to one of Brute Wilger's legs and one of his arms, ending by getting toes and fingers in such a position that he could hold the Brute helpless with one hand. The Brute tried to move once and knew excruciating pain—and did not try again.

"Should you attempt violence again, I shall feel compelled to deal harshly with you," the professor warned him. "I now am going to let you up and conduct you to my little study. We are going to have a conversation there."

Brute Wilger got up when the professor allowed it. There was admiration and respect in the Brute's face. He had a reputation as a gangster and a brutal man, but he knew he was as helpless as a babe in the hands of Prof. Salwick. He sat in the chair the professor indicated and wiped the perspiration from his forehead with the back of one dirty hand.

"Make yourself comfortable," said Prof. Salwick. "I long have wished to meet a criminal. I have seen many of them in court, of course, and in police stations—but I wanted to see one at work. I have made quite a study of criminology, but I feel that much of my data and incorrect. I shall expect you to speak the truth during our conversation."

"I don't quite get this," said Brute Wilger.

"How long have you expressed your criminal tendencies in actual acts of crime?"

"Meaning how long have I been a crook?"

"I believe that is the accepted term."

"What is this—the third degree?"

"I have not the slightest connection with the police," said the professor. "In fact, I abhor them. The police, to my way of thinking, are human beings of deep ignorance. Their methods are neither scientific nor resultant in good."

"I guess we can agree on that," said the Brute.

"So you may talk freely to me. It is information I wish. If you give it to me, you shall be rewarded—with money."

"Well, I've been followin' the game for about ten years," Brute Wilger said frankly.

"And yet you made an attempt to rob my apartment tonight! I am a college professor, and there is little in my place that would attract a criminal who wished for illegal gain. I have a small fortune, it is true, left me by a relative, but it is out at interest. Are you a successful criminal?"

"Oh, I guess I've pulled down about $5,000 a year, all right."

"You have averaged $5,000 a year? Young man, I am a scientist of wide reputation, I work hard and study continually, and my remuneration is $2,500 a year."

"Gosh!"

"I have been studying criminals and criminology for some years, I have read all the fiction of that sort that is published. It has come to my mind that most criminals fail because they do not use their brains. As to the question of right and wrong, that does not trouble me. A scientist such as myself is above the law. For some time I have been contemplating a certain step, and I feel that this—er—visit of yours points to me the way—"

"I don't quite get this!" said the Brute.

"Crime as a business should lead to rich rewards, especially at this time when the average peace officer is a man of but ordinary intelligence. I have studied, I may remark, the methods of criminals and policemen, and there are glaring errors in both. If a man in excellent physical condition applied science to thievery, he would undoubtedly outwit his foes. The adventure would be commensurate with the monetary reward, also. May I ask your name?"

"I ain't mentionin' names," Brute Wilger said quickly and with sudden suspicion.

"Quite so! I can understand your reluctance, of course. But I assure you that I have no ulterior motive in asking. We may meet again soon, under different circumstances, and I then should like to renew our acquaintance begun so happily tonight."

"Where'll we ever meet again?" the Brute asked.

"Who knows? Perhaps in some dark corner of that peculiar country designated as the underworld. I feel that I have come to the bank of a sort of Rubicon—and this very day I shall hurl myself into the flood and swing to the other shore. I intend to give up my classes and become a criminal."

II

An Unfair Fight

"R ed" Riley, disregarding warnings given him by certain gentlemen connected with the police, had dared travel uptown and steal a purse.

The picking of pockets was only a sideline with "Red" Riley, who was known to the underworld professionally as a burglar, a gangster, and a thug. He picked pockets only when funds were needed to tide him over until a "crib" could be "cracked."

Having picked the pocket while in the midst of a jostling theater crowd, "Red" Riley—the "leather" still in his possession—had observed the approach of a city detective to whom he was well known.

Into the subway he darted and was fortunate enough to board an express for downtown immediately. Far downtown, he left the train and ascended to the street. He hurried for half a dozen blocks until he had reached a dark cross-street well known to him and his kind.

Certainly, it was an unfortunate sight. Approaching him was another city detective to whom he was known. Riley could not continue along the street without running into the detective and danger; he could not retreat swiftly without attracting attention and rousing suspicion and causing pursuit. He came to the mouth of a poorly lighted alley, and darted down it.

Here and there in the alley were little doors with dirty electric light bulbs glowing over them. "Red" Riley knew them for what they were—side entrances to cheap saloons, cheaper lodging-houses. His only chance of immediate escape, he knew, would be to enter one of the doors before the detective reached the mouth of the alley.

He did not hesitate. He opened the first door and darted inside, closing the door softly behind him. And then he whirled around and regarded the interior of the place.

He saw instantly that he had made a sad mistake, that this was not the place he would have selected, had there been time to make a selection. Being a gangster, "Red" Riley had foes—and he had invaded one of their dens.

Mean, snarling faces were before him. He found himself in a little room where there were a dozen cheap tables scattered around. The walls were stained with liquor, the place reeked with tobacco smoke, the floor was half covered with dirt.

"Red" Riley gulped once and then stepped away

from the door and into the brighter light. Voices had ceased upon his entrance; these men merely glanced at him, waited for word or his action.

A soft voice came from the corner of the room. "Moll buzzer!"

There was a wealth of disgust in the two words. "Red" Riley was a gangster, a burglar, a man of parts in the underworld. And to call him a "moll buzzer," a robber of women, a man without courage enough to steal from other men, was the limit of insult as "Red" Riley understood it.

He whirled angrily, his face flaming again, his chin thrust out, his eyes glittering like those of a snake.

"If that crack was made at me," he snapped, "suppose the gent that made it stands up and lets me get a good look at his ugly mug!"

There was silence for an instant, and then a chair scraped against the floor again, and a man stood up. He was "Shifty" Slade, gang chief, the most cruel and most formidable in the city.

Slade walked forward to within ten feet of him, his fists upon his hips, a sneer upon his face.

"I made the crack, Riley!" he said. "And I made it straight at you. I say you're a moll buzzer, a guy with no nerve, a third-rate dip tryin' to pose as a burglar. And I'm waitin' to see what you're goin' to do about it!"

That meant fight. One of the gangsters rushed to the alley door to prevent outsiders entering; two others hurried to the swinging doors for the same reason. "Red" Riley hurled his cap to the floor, -

bellowed like a bull, and launched himself forward.

He had not expected to have an easy time of it, and he did not. "Shifty" Slade was a match for him physically. They entered in the middle of the room, and Slade's one shout to his friends was to the effect that this was his personal fight, a duel between gang leaders, and that he was not asking for help and did not expect any to be offered.

For five minutes it endured, and then Slade began to give ground a little.

Riley caught the flash of a knife. He grappled with his man, seized his wrist and beat it across one of his knees, trying to break it. He did not succeed, but Slade dropped the knife, and it clattered to the floor.

The gangsters were murmuring louder now, and Riley knew by glancing at their faces that they did not take kindly to seeing their new leader beaten. There would be no shooting, Riley knew—for these men did not carry revolvers or automatics unless they were out to perform certain work. But they had knives and could use them. Riley did not doubt that any man in that room would hand Slade another knife if he got the opportunity. He caught Slade again, bent him backward, smashed his fist at the man's face. The growls of those against Riley was increased; they snarled and drew closer. And then they rushed!

"Red" Riley hurled Slade against the foremost of them, checking their advance, but the others rushed on. They piled against him, tried to overwhelm him, tried to get in blows with fists and knives. Riley supposed that this was to be the end. He was fighting a losing battle, he knew.

And then somebody hurled himself through the swinging doors past the two guards who had bee stationed there. Riley glanced in that direction, hoping almost against hope that it would be one of his own gang. But he saw a medium-sized man who wore spectacles and who was dressed like a merchant of small means, and his momentary hope died.

"Smash into them!" the newcomer said. "A dozen against one is unfair odds! I shall assist you!"

He was at "Red" Riley's side as he finished speaking, and his fists were working like twin pistons. He drove back Riley's foes and urged the staggering Riley toward the door.

They reached the door, and the mysterious newcomer hurled the gangster guard to one side. Now they were out in the alley, and the cool air struck upon them and seemed to give them strength anew. But he gangsters were not done; they continued to crowd forward, carrying on the battle, fighting almost silently. And Riley and his new comrade retreated slowly, stopping now and then to fight back a rush, guarding always against a knife thrust in the alley's semigloom.

III

Recruits for a Cause

Back they went, foot by foot, fighting and disputing every inch of the way. They came to a flight of three or four steps that ran up to a door, and up them they dashed, for it gave them some slight advantage of position. And there they fought, as the gangsters charged from the front and from either side.

And then it happened—the thing for which "Red" Riley and his companion had not been looking. They might have guessed that the door at the top of that little flight of steps led into the rear hall of a lodging house, but they had given no thought to it, except that "Red" Riley had tried it first and had found it locked.

And now the door was thrown open suddenly. Riley had been leaning against it, bracing himself, and so had his companion. They tottered and sprawled backwards, inside. The door was slammed shut again and their foes barred out.

Riley looked at the woman who stood before them— rubbed his eyes and looked again. She was of medium size, dressed in an evening gown, jewels glittering on her fingers. Over her face was a black mask. "Red" Riley felt sure that she was not woman of his acquaintance. And he wondered what she was doing in such a place, and why she wore the mask, and why she had rescued him and the man who wore the spectacles.

Riley started to gasp his thanks. But his companion was before him.

"My dear madam," he said, "I fail to find words strong enough to thank you for what you have done. We were in perilous straits. Another five minuets, and those wolves would have devoured us."

"Come this way, please," the woman said.

She walked down the hall, and they staggered weakly after her. They came to a stairwell and went up one flight, and there the masked woman opened a door and ushered them into a room.

"Red" Riley gasped when they entered. It was furnished lavishly and in excellent taste. There was a piano; there were books, pictures. Through an open door could be seen another room furnished similarly. Riley rubbed at his eyes again.

"Allow me to thank you once more, madam," the voice of his companion came to him. "And allow me to introduce myself. I am Prof. James Xenophon Salwick, holding the chair of physics in the university, and an authority on anthropology. My young friend is known, I believe, as "Red" Riley.

"The gangsters attacked this young man in a dive in the alley, and I went to his assistance," the professor continued. "It was not from a pure motive of gallantry however. I had an axe to grind, as the saying goes."

"Indeed!"

"A few days ago, I determined to become a professional criminal. I have been searching for a pal—I believe that is the term? It came to my mind, when I saw the combat begin, that, if I gave assistance to this young man, he would be grateful enough to combine forces with me in my endeavors."

"I'll stand by you any time, old scout!" "Red" Riley said. "And believe me, you'll need it. That man I fought was "Shifty" Slade, and he most of the others belong to his gang."

"'Shifty' Slade!" the woman gasped. "You fought him? Oh! Let me thank you for that, Mr. Riley!"

"You're mighty free with my name, but I don't remember of hearin' yours," Riley said, quick suspicion in his eyes.

"You may call me Mme. Madcap—many persons do."

Riley was breathing normally now and the lust of battle had left him. He was alert again, keen, every sense on edge, once more the careful, cunning "Red" Riley who had led his gangsters to so many victories.

"Well, thanks for helpin' us out," he said, "and now I guess I'll slide. There's a front door to this dump, I suppose."

"If you'll sit down—for just a moment," Mme. Madcap begged. "Thank you! I shall try to explain. I saw the attack in the alley, and was eager to rescue you. You perhaps are mystified at my appearance and especially the mask. I put it on before opening the door for you because I did not know your identities, you see."

"Quite right, Mme. Madcap—you did quite right!" said the professor.

"Why should a jane want to hide her face?" Riley asked. "I wouldn't mind takin' a peek at it myself."

"Perhaps you may—under certain conditions," Mme. Madcap said. "For I am going to make you an offer. Mr. Riley. You are a gangster—I have heard your name often. And you, Prof. Salwick, call yourself a criminal. You are eccentric, I make bold to say—but perhaps you are playing a new and deep game. At least I suspect as much. Now, so that we may understand one another, let me say that I am a criminal myself."

"Never heard of you!" Riley sneered.

"Have you ever been in Paris?" she asked.

"No."

"Possibly that explains it."

"Ah!" the professor cried. "I see it now! You are one of those clever continental women of whom I have read. You play the game of strategy and wit! Clever, clever woman! If there is any way in which we can serve you—"

"I am starting work in this city," she replied. "I have very few associates yet, and I am looking for recruits. There will be plenty of profit, I assure you.

And there will be fame for you in the underworld, too, for within a short time the name of Mme. Madcap will be known well throughout the city.

"Nothing could be more appropriate," said the professor. "I shall be pleased to ally myself with you."

"Well, I ain't turnin' down any good bets!" Riley said. "Let's get down to cases."

"It is very simple," Mme. Madcap said. "You are to trust me, of course. You are to accept my commands and execute them loyally. And you are not to ask questions!"

"I don't jump off any roof blindfolded!" "Red" Riley told her. "You may be a female copper for all I know."

"I can tell you this," Mme. Madcap said. "I have a mission to perform. It has to do with certain men who must be punished—and some who are to be robbed. Do you know Hamilton Brone?"

"I know the man," the professor said. "He is a young millionaire who wastes oceans of money on frivolities. I at one time asked him to endow a chair of anthropology in our institution. The confounded rascal told me that he needed all his funds for the rearing of fancy chickens. I ascertained afterward that he spoke a falsehood—he has no chicken farm, or anything of the sort."

"He's got a chicken farm, all right—pastures 'em in the cabarets," "Red" Riley said.

"Hamilton Brone is concerned in my enterprise," Mme. Madcap told them.

"If you're out to pluck that guy, and there's a

chance of doin' it, I'm in!" Riley said.

Mme. Madcap raised her hands and removed her mask. Prof. Salwick uttered a little cry of delight, and "Red" Riley gasped his admiration.

She probably was twenty-four. Her features were regular, charming. There was an adorable dimple just where a dimple should nestle against the chin. Her eyes were blue and her hair almost golden.

"It's bunk!" Riley exclaimed. "You ain't any more a crook then a preacher's wife could be! With that face? Professor, if you want to hook up with this jane, you go right ahead and do it. I'm goin' to walk out the front door of this buildin' and go about my business."

"I regret that I cannot allow that," Mme. Madcap said. "You have seen my face and have heard a little of my plans. I cannot allow you to go now, knowing as much as you do."

"What's to stop me?" "Red" Riley asked.

Mme. Madcap raised her voice.

"Sambo!" she called.

There entered from an adjoining room, immediately, the largest black man "Red" Riley had ever seen. His face was that of a brute. His gnarled hands were massive; there were roils of muscles on his arms and shoulders, and he towered over six feet tall.

"Sambo," said Mme. Madcap, "do you see that man in the chair at the end of the table?"

She pointed a forefinger at "Red" Riley, and Sambo nodded that he saw.

"He does not wish to join us, Sambo, and I desire

him to do so," she continued. "He will understand later, and possibly be glad. But just now he wishes to leave, and I cannot allow it."

"He won't leave, miss," Sambo said.

IV

A New Sensation

"R ed" Riley's eyes bulged, and he measured the distance to the door, deciding instantly that he could not reach it if Sambo essayed to prevent him. The giant black man extended his half closed hands a few inches, as if about to grasp something by the throat and choke the life out of it, and grinned.

"Man," Sambo said, "I've got my oders, and I'm going to carry 'em out. You'd better submit, man! Don't you rile me, or I'm liable to get violent!"

"Keep away from me!" "Red" Riley exclaimed. "You put your paws on me, and I'll make hash out of you!"

He sprang for the door, for Sambo had moved a few feet away from it. He reached it—and felt his feet leave the floor. "Red" Riley realized that the giant had lifted him bodily.

Though still weak from his battle in the alley, "Red" Riley was not the man to submit without opposition in such an emergency. He attempted to kick and strike, and merely succeeded in exhausting himself. Sambo tucked him beneath one arm, held both his wrists in the grasp of one hand, dragged his feet on the floor, and so carried him into the hallway.

The giant carried "Red" Riley speedily along the hall, up another flight of stairs, and opened a door. Still holding Riley beneath his arm, the man reached for a switch and turned on the electric lights.

"Red" Riley gasped in mingled terror and surprise. The room was enough to make his insides squirm. It was of medium size, and there was not a bit of furniture in it. But, in the center, were two steel cages about eight feet square, each supplied with an iron bunk and a metal stool. "Red" Riley, who had been incarcerated a few times, shuddered. The cages certainly looked like detention cells.

Sambo threw "Red" Riley into one of the little cells, slammed and locked the door, and put the key into his pocket. Then he snapped out the lights and departed. "Red" Riley heard the key turned in the lock of the outer door.

On the floor below, Prof. Salwick was in close conversation with Mme. Madcap.

"It is my wish that you do these things I have told you," she said, "and ask no questions about it at the present time. You are willing?"

"More than willing—delighted." Prof. Salwick assured her.

"And you are to forget that you are a criminal

while in the presence of other persons, of course. A great deal depends upon our work tonight. I have been prepared for some time, but had almost despaired of getting the proper man for the task until good fortune brought you to my door."

"Say, rather, that it was my good fortune to be rescued by such a charming woman," the professor replied. "But one thing troubles me—I shall have to have evening dress. I have retained my apartment uptown, of course, though engaging a room in the—er—nefarious district. Or may a district be nefarious? No matter!"

"We have ample time," said Mme. Madcap. "We shall drive to your apartment, and then I'll drive through the part while you are dressing."

She touched a bell on the table, and Sambo appeared.

"How about Mr. Riley?" she asked.

"He is thinkin' it ovah."

"Very well. We'll start in five minutes," said Mme. Madcap.

Sambo disappeared. Mme. Madcap took up the mask and fixed it over her face again. It was a serviceable mask, and its lines were such that they destroyed identity effectually.

"There is another matter," she said. "I speak of it now just to get it fixed in your mind. There is a man name Brute Wilger; I want you to locate him later. Also a man known as 'Gentleman Joe' Marget. You already have met 'Shifty' Slade. I shall have to smooth over your trouble with him. You see, professor, I want those three men in my organization."

Mme. Madcap glanced at the clock on the wall.

"I think that it is time for us to go," she said.

They went to the lower floor, along the hall there, and came to a little door which Mme. Madcap opened. The professor saw before him a narrow, dark passage. Through this he followed Mme. Madcap for a distance of fifty feet, and then she flashed an electric torch. Before them was another door, and beside it, a woman's long cloak on a hook. Mme. Madcap took the cloak down, and Prof. Salwick held it for her. Then she unlocked and opened the door.

They emerged into an alley less than twenty feet from the side street where a limousine stood at the curb. Sambo was holding the door open. They hurried along the wall, across the walk, and sprang into the limousine. Sambo went in front and got behind the wheel. Mme. Madcap gave him the address of the apartment house where the professor had his rooms.

Once there, the professor hurried inside, his heart fluttering at the romance of it and the unusual haste, and Mme. Madcap had Sambo drive her around the park for half an hour. At the end of that time, the limousine stopped before the apartment house again, and the professor got in, carrying a suitcase.

"I shall keep evening clothes at my downtown address hereafter," he explained.

"Very good. You'll have need of evening dress regularly for some time," Mme. Madcap answered.

Sambo, who had his orders, drove quickly

through the well-lit streets and finally drew up before the brilliant entrance of a famous café. The professor and Mme. Madcap stepped out. Sambo drove the limousine a few yards away from the café entrance and stopped at the curb.

Prof. Salwick knew little about cafés. Two or three times in his career he had visited such places, but generally those of the quieter sort, and only for afternoon tea. But he threw back his shoulders, glared at the doorman, and with Mme. Madcap on his arm, stepped inside briskly.

The professor handed his hat and coat and Mme. Madcap's cloak to the check boy. And then Prof. Salwick offered his arm again, and Mme. Madcap accepted it, and they swept past the astonished clerks and flower girls and into the main room of the café.

V

A Queer Statement

Piloted by the head waiter, the professor and Mme. Madcap walked around the edge of the dancing floor and were shown to a table near one corner of it. They made themselves comfortable, and Prof. Salwick, remembering his instructions and the roll of bills in his pocket given him by Mme. Madcap, ordered rich food and drink.

Mme. Madcap had been taken, at first, for one of the entertainers. But it needed only a second glance to convince most of those in the room to the contrary. The food and wine arrived, and they ate and drank. Mme. Madcap looked around the room as though oblivious of the sensation she had caused already. The professor began to fidget.

"What is the next move in our little game?" he asked after a time.

"The public makes the next move—we do not,"

Mme. Madcap told him. "And just now, I want you to call the waiter and send for the professional dancer."

Prof. Salwick beckoned the waiter, who called the professional to the table. The latter was more than eager to dance with the unknown masked lady who gave every hint of being beautiful as well as graceful. And he was a famous and particular professional who danced only with partners of his own choosing.

"New entertainer!" whispered the regular patrons. "Just a new trick! Bunk! But she certainly can dance!"

Back at the table again, Mme. Madcap thanked the professional prettily, said that she did not care to dance again just then but might do so on another occasion, and then sipped her wine as if the eyes of every person in the room were not upon her. The elated professor immediately found himself a great favorite.

Gentlemen without escort hailed the dancer and piled him with questions.

"No, she isn't an entertainer!" the dancer said. "She's not employed here at all. I never saw her before. She said to call her Mme. Madcap. She might have an ugly face under that mask, or a face that's been burned or something like that—but she sure can dance. Take it from one who knows!"

Mme. Madcap again was looking slowly around the café, and presently she bent nearer Prof. Salwick and whispered.

"Look at the table straight across—behind that woman with the pink dress."

The professor looked.

"Hamilton Brone!" he whispered in reply.

"Yes. Do you know the man at table with him?"

"I do not."

"He is Wallace Melkington. Look at him well, but do not let either of them suspect that we are watching them. Be sure that you'll know Hamilton Brone and Wallace Melkington any time you may see them."

"I never forget a face," the professor said.

"Very well. Leave me now, and go into the foyer on some pretext. You remember the remainder of my instructions for the evening?"

"I have not forgotten a word of them, Mme. Madcap, I assure you. I shall carry them out."

Prof. Salwick arose, excused himself, and walked around the edge of the dancing floor toward the foyer. He reached the end of the foyer and turned back, and somebody touched him on the arm. It was Hamilton Brone.

"Isn't this Prof. Salwick of the university?" Brone asked.

"I am," the professor admitted.

"Don't you remember me?"

"You are Hamilton Brone," the professor replied. "I once endeavored to get you to endow a chair of anthropology, and you replied that you needed all your money for the rearing of fancy chickens."

Brone laughed heartily; so did Wallace Melkington, who was just behind him. Brone introduced Melkington, and the three men stepped to one side.

"Perhaps I may give you money for the chair of anthropology yet," Brone said.

"It would be a blessing," Prof. Salwick replied.

"I don't believe I ever noticed you here before."

"I've never been here before," said the professor, "but I am liable to be here frequently now."

"Pardon me, but why is your charming companion masked?" Brone asked.

"That is a secret."

Brone looked at Melkington and closed one eye slowly. "Some of those fellows are not good medicine for a charming young lady. If you care to introduce Mr. Melkington and myself, we'll be delighted to dance with her."

"I'm not sure she'd dance," the professor replied.

"Why not introduce us and let us find out?" Brone persisted.

"Wouldn't it make you conspicuous if you danced with her?"

"It wouldn't startle the natives if they saw Brone do something conspicuous," Melkington said, laughing.

"And I may remember about that chair of anthropology," Brone said. "Especially if you tell me something about her before you introduce us."

"I can tell you very little," Professor Salwick declared. He was remembering what Mme. Madcap had told him to say. "If you find out anything, it will have to be from her."

"Can't you at least tell us her name?"

"Mme. Madcap."

"Her real name, confound it!" Brone said.

"Against the rules," said the professor, puffing furiously at his cigar. "Let me intimate this much to you: When college is not is session, I earn needed funds by tutoring—er—taking odd jobs of a peculiar nature. I have a modest fortune, but it is out at interest, and I am always needing money for books and apparatus."

"I understand," said Brone.

"And though I never have hired myself as an escort before—"

"So that is it? A hired escort for a mysterious woman!" Melkington exclaimed.

"And I really know very little about her, and what I do know, I have promised to keep secret!" the professor declared. "I'll introduce you—and please do not forget about the chair of anthropology."

He tossed away his cigar and led the others back into the main room and along the edge of the dancing floor. He introduced Brone and Melkington to Mme. Madcap, and they sat down.

"You are the sensation of the season already, Mme. Madcap," Brone told her.

"Simply because I wear a mask?" she asked.

"That is a part, of course—but your grace and beauty—"

"I may be as ugly as an ogre," she said.

"Not with that voice—you couldn't be!" Brone declared.

"Nor with that laugh," added Melkington, as Mme. Madcap laughed lightly.

"I may be some woman you both know," she said.

"There is no woman of my acquaintance half so charming," Melkington declared.

"And I am sure I never saw you before," said Brone. "Will you dance with me?"

The music was starting. Mme. Madcap seemed to hesitate for an instant, and then she got up, and Brone clasped her in his arms and swung her onto the dancing floor. Once more the buzz of excited conversation ran around the café. Hamilton Brone, whose affairs were countless and notorious, was dancing with the mysterious masked beauty!

"I must learn your identity," Brone was whispering in her ear.

"That will prove difficult," she said.

"But I may try?"

"Oh, I give you permission to try," she answered. "Try in every way you like. But why should you be so eager to know?"

Brone did not reply; he merely pressed her closer. Brone was susceptible where pretty women were concerned, and this masked beauty seemed to intoxicate him. There was a subtle perfume about her; she danced like a woman with wings, and her whispered words made Brone's blood tingle.

The dance ended, and the infatuated Hamilton Brone returned her to the table. Then she danced with Wallace Melkington.

Brone might have been displeased had he been behind them as they danced. Mme. Madcap exerted all her wiles upon Melkington, too, and before the dance ended he, also, was infatuated. And then they were back at the table again, the glasses were filled with fresh wine, and Mme. Madcap was speaking.

"If you are a bit interested, you must make me some promise," she said. "You are never to presume upon this evening's acquaintance to approach me. If we meet again, you are to remain away unless I beckon you to my side."

"Why be so cruel?" Brone asked.

"If you do not obey, I shall refuse to recognize you. If you are good, perhaps I may dance with you again."

"But are we not to know your true name?" Brone asked.

"That would spoil everything," Mme. Madcap said. "Learn it—if you can. And now you must run away. I mean it—you must run away!"

She forced them to take their leave. And when they had returned to their own table, she bent nearer Prof. Salwick and whispered.

"Everything is starting our right," she said. "But how I do hate those two men! See—they are watching us now! They'll not take their eyes off us, and they'll try to find out where I live. Well, I am prepared for that!"

"There is another man at their table now," said the professor.

Mme. Madcap glanced across the dancing floor.

"That is one man we may have reason to fear!" she whispered. "Look at him and remember his face. He is a particular friend of Hamilton Brone and of Mrs. Brone. That, my dear professor, is Lionel Waldron, the famous private detective."

"Ah! A real foe!"

"He may prove to be soon. He is looking this way now— Hamilton Brone and Wallace Melkington are telling him about me."

The professor rubbed his hands together nervously.

"Are you not—er—a bit afraid?" he questioned.

"Afraid?" She laughed again. "My dear professor, I certainly am not afraid. My plans are perfect. If my mask were off and he had a good enough look at my face to identify me, I could still convince any honest jury tomorrow, by reliable witness, that I had not been in this café tonight!"

VI

Riley Succumbs

The orchestra ceased playing, the dancers left the floor, the lights were turned low again, and a section of the cabaret performances began.

"Now is the time for us to make our escape," Mme. Madcap whispered. "Call the waiter and pay the check, and then let us walk around the edge of the dancing floor, behind the first row of tables. I hope to get away without Hamilton Brone seeing. I wanted to have him meet me, and arouse his curiosity, but that is as far as I wish it to go at the present time. If we can escape, he will be all the more eager to see me again."

Mme. Madcap's ruse was successful, and they reached the waiting limousine without being followed. For Brone, meanwhile was unsuccessfully attempting to enlist Lionel Waldron's aid in discovering the identity of the masked woman.

"Name your own price, Waldron!" he argued. "I want to find out all about that woman—her name and address—all about her."

"I don't care to take the case," Waldron said coldly. "I'm not a preacher, Ham, but it seems to me you have been going at it a bit of late. And you have a wife who—"

"I know!" Brone interrupted. "You think my wife is the greatest woman in the world. But she turned you down and married me."

"Brone!"

"I didn't mean to say that. But it should make no difference to you if I get interested in another woman now and then. I'm talking business to you. You are a professional detective, and I want to engage your services."

"And they are not for sale in the present instance," Lionel Waldron replied. "I'm not in the habit of aiding libertines in their amours for a fee!"

"The first adventure has ended well," Mme. Madcap said when they had reached the house. "Come into the parlor, professor, and rest for a few minutes. There is a room upstairs for you to use. If you have another room rented, move your things from it tomorrow. I want all my people here with me."

"Isn't that—er—dangerous?" The professor asked.

"Not at all. I have a friend who will be here in the morning, and she will pose as a landlady of a lodging house. It goes without saying, of course, that her rooms will be full if strangers attempt to rent one. I own the house."

"I think that you are a remarkable woman!" Prof. Salwick exclaimed. "But if you will pardon me, we do not seem to have done anything criminal this evening."

"We are preparing," Mme. Madcap said. "And now let us send for Mr. Riley."

Unlocking the cell door, Sambo tucked "Red" Riley beneath one arm, held his two wrists with one hand, carried him down stairs to the parlor, put him down, and then stepped back to the door to stand guard.

"I've had about enough of this!" "Red" Riley snarled.

Mme. Madcap motioned him to a chair beside the table, but Riley announced that he preferred to stand.

Mme. Madcap had taken a purse from her bosom, a purse of the sort one uses for bills only. Now, as the eyes of "Red" Riley bulged and those of Prof. Salwick blinked rapidly, she opened the purse and took out a sheaf of currency. They could see that the sheaf consisted of hundred-dollar bills.

"I suppose money talks with you, Mr. "Red" Riley," she said. "I know your type, and I know that you'll join me if you think there is enough money in it. You'll get your share of the profits if you work with me, stand loyal to me, and do as I command—and ask no questions. Here are two hundred-dollar bills, Mr. Riley. I am putting them on the table before you. If you pick them up and put them into your own pockets, you are my man."

"Red" Riley licked his lips and regarded the crisp new bills on the table before him. He hesitated a moment longer, ran his fingers around the inside of his collar, gulped, and then extended a hand and picked up the two bills.

"I'm your man!" he announced. "When do I eat?"

VII

Waldron Makes a Mistake

Having joined forces with Mme. Madcap, "Red" Riley thought of nothing except serving her well and being a loyal subject. Therefore, he spent several days and a great deal of Mme. Madcap's money in some peculiar publicity work. And there was considerable speculations when "Red" Riley appeared with plenty of money in his pockets and disposition to spend it, which meant to his friends that there was more where that had come from.

Riley was secretive at first. He assured the members of his own gang that he was working in another group for a time, but with people not opposed to their interests.

"This stuff is class—get me!" he said. "The crowd I'm workin' with is not ordinary gang. And I'm rememberin' my pals. Maybe I'll be able to get some of you in on somethin' soft before long. But the crowd is class, I'm sayin'!"

Riley distributed expensive cigarettes with a lavish hand to the aggregation that had been listening and then broke away and swung through the door of a local restaurant as if he owned the building, sat down at a table, and waited for the proper sort of audience.

His heart skipped a beat as the doors were swung open again and another man entered. "Red" Riley knew him. He belonged to the gang headed by "Shifty" Slade. His name was "Gentleman Joe" Marget.

There was no dodging Marget at this time, and "Red" Riley did not care to do so. It was mid-afternoon, and this resort was a neutral place, not dominated by any gang. So Riley rolled a cigarette, lighted it, puffed it a few times, and looked up. "Gentleman Joe" Marget stood beside the table, his face inscrutable.

"Hello!" "Red" Riley said.

Marget's eyes narrowed, and without invitation, he sat down across the table from Riley. He bent across it, his hands before him to show that he did not intend to make a hostile move.

"I understand you've given out that you've quit the old gang," he remarked.

"I have not! I'm merely workin' somethin' else for a few days. I don't quit my pals."

"Hooked up with a highbrow outfit, have you? Well, I can't say that I blame you," Marget said. "I get mighty tired of the Slade crowd sometimes."

"Ever tell him that?"

"Oh, I'm not particularly afraid of Slade," Marget told him. "It isn't Slade's gang, really. It was old Bill Duncan's gang, and Slade just stepped in and took charge when Bill Duncan was sent away for twenty-five mileposts."

"Well, ain't that all right?"

"You don't get me," Marget said. "Bill Duncan was what the cops called a master-criminal. He planned stunts and we carried them out, and there was a certain amount of profit and glory."

"You needn't tell me the history of the Duncan gang," Riley said. "Everybody knows it."

"And since Duncan was put away, Slade has tried to change things," Marget continued. "Duncan had brains. Slade's a scrapper. The old Duncan gang is being made into a bunch of common corner gangsters."

"Why don't you pull out?" Riley asked.

"I want to. But I can't simply throw down the gang and join another that we've been fighting. And I don't want to be left out in the cold. A man's got to live, and I never did have any luck working alone. Now I understand that you're hooked up with some new and classy crowd that isn't fighting any gang. If I could get into something like that—"

"Well, you're a good man in your line of work," Riley said. "I'll whisper to the boss about it and let you know."

"Who is the boss?"

"She calls herself Mme. Madcap," Riley said.

"A woman?"

"She certainly is, and a chicken for looks. But don't get the idea she doesn't know the game, bo! If you knew the irons she's got in the fire now—oh, son!"

"Gentleman Joe" Marget betrayed sudden interest. When he parted from "Red" Riley ten minutes later, it was understood that there was to be a sort of armed neutrality between them. Riley, being a gangster, always made it a point to take a good man from a rival gang when possible. It was good policy to weaken the foe. But "Red" Riley always was most careful about it.

During these days, the professor was like a man in a whirlwind. His principal duty, it appeared, was to be Mme. Madcap's escort to the café each evening. And this pleased the professor, who appreciated, also, the neat game Mme. Madcap was playing.

The professor knew only that it was her intention to get Hamilton Brone infatuated with her. Before three visits had been made to the café, he realized that Wallace Melkington was to be a victim, too. Mme. Madcap had not explained exactly what she intended doing, and the professor did not ask.

Brone and Melkington continued their attempts to learn Mme. Madcap's identify, and there had been another effort to bribe Sambo, which resulted in failure. Mme. Madcap played the game well. She danced with Hamilton Brone, occasionally, and with Melkington. When she beckoned, they rushed to her side; and they departed at her command.

She was a sensation, of course. Devotees of the bright lights were whispering about the mysterious masked woman who appeared at the café every night, and it was an open scandal that Hamilton Brone was infatuated, and Melkington also.

Lionel Waldron talked to Brone on occasion, but to no effect. Their last interview had almost ended in fisticuffs, and Waldron had decided to leave Brone alone. But he knew Brone's wife, having been a rejected suitor, and respected her enough to want to save Brone from making a fool of himself in public.

So it happened that, on a certain evening, Mme. Madcap and the professor had no more than settled themselves comfortably at their usual table when a waiter brought Mme. Madcap a note. She gave the professor a peculiar look, then opened it and read.

"This grows interesting," she whispered across the table. "The note is from Lionel Waldron, the aristocratic private detective. He says he wishes to talk to me about a certain matter."

"And what are my orders on this occasion?"

"I'll send for him. As soon as he comes, you are to leave and take a stroll around the foyer. Watch me and be ready to return when I signal you."

Mme. Madcap gave the waiter his instructions. A few minutes later, Lionel Waldron stopped beside the table and bowed to her.

The professor excused himself and hurried away.

"And what was it that you wished to speak to me about, Mr. Waldron?" Mme. Madcap asked in her rich voice. "If you have come to ask me to dance—"

"It is not that, I assure you," Waldron hastened to say. "I going to speak very frankly, madam. There is a certain gentleman infatuated with you. I'll not say you have been encouraging him, but he does not need much encouragement."

"I suppose you mean Mr. Melkington?"

"I mean Hamilton Brone," Waldron replied.

"I have talked with Mr. Brone a few times, and danced with him once or twice."

"You have started in to captivate the man, and you are doing it deliberately," Waldron accused. "You are conspicuous, of course, and the fact that Hamilton Brone is infatuated with you is making him the laughingstock of the town. It has reached his wife's ears."

"Then it is a question of her pride being bruised?" Mme. Madcap asked. "I suppose it is commendable of you to have this interview with me, but really I cannot see that it is any of your business."

The bank of foliage and bloom behind the table parted, and Hamilton Brone stepped up to the table.

"You're right—it isn't any of his business!" he said.

They turned to face him. Hamilton Brone had been taking too much wine. His face was flushed more than usual, his eyes were bulging, he was breathing deeply. He was in a dangerous mood, and Lionel Waldron knew it, knowing the man as he did. He would have gone away after a soft word or two, but Hamilton Brone was not content to have it that way.

"You're concerning yourself too much in my affairs, Waldron," he said. "Can't a gentleman have a few friends without all his wife's rejected suitors pestering the life out of him?"

Melkington had been behind Brone. And now he stepped forward and touched him on the arm.

"Easy!" Melkington said. "Come away now, Hamilton!"

Brone whirled upon him with a snarl like that of an angry beast, a drunken, nasty snarl that showed the man's true character as nothing else could have done.

"You'd like to have me go away, wouldn't you?" he sneered. "Like to get me away and try to get ahead of me with the lady who wears the mask, eh? You're my friend, are you?"

"Hamilton!"

"Shut up! I'm a bit sick of having you trot at my heels all the time, at that!"

Melkington had been drinking, too. Anger flared in his face and his voice was charged with passion.

"Don't talk to me like that!" he hissed.

"Then get out! I don't want you around me!" Brone said, speaking louder than before.

Guests at half a dozen tables heard the words and noted Brone's manner. Melkington realized it. He trembled with rage, and he took a step nearer the table when he spoke.

"I'll get you for that!" he snarled. "You can't insult me in public and get away with it!"

He whirled around and was gone. Brone looked after him, still sneering. Then he turned to face Lionel Waldron again. Two waiters were approaching the table, fearing trouble and ready to cope with it.

But Waldron had no ambition to figure in a scene before the throng in the café. Without a word more to other Mme. Madcap or Hamilton Brone, he turned and walked along the edge of the dancing floor, going toward the foyer.

"Sit down, Hamilton," Mme. Madcap said. "Do you want them to throw me out of the café?"

It was the first time Mme. Madcap had used his given name, and it thrilled Brone. He sank into the nearest chair and bent toward her.

"Even you don't play fair," he said. "You still run away from me. You won't let me know where you live, who you are—won't let me see your face. I'm crazy about you, and you know it. And I'm not treated right!"

"Perhaps I'll treat you fairly if you'll behave yourself."

"Well, what do you want me to do now?"

"Leave and go to the bar or somewhere—and don't quarrel with Wallace Melkington again. Don't stay too long—watch. I'll leave the café about the usual time. And I'll get rid of my escort before I go."

"And then—" Brone asked, bending closer to her.

"Watch when I leave—and get into the limousine with me," she whispered.

"You mean it?" he gasped.

"Stay away from Melkington. But if you want to show Waldron that he can't run a man like you, let him know that you're going with me—let him see us leave."

"I'll do it! I'll do it!" Brone said.

"Go away now! The professor will be coming back. I'll have to get rid of him, you know."

Half an hour later, Detective Lionel Waldron saw the professor leave the café. And hour later, he saw Hamilton Brone and Mme. Madcap get into the latter's limousine and drive away.

Thereupon, Lionel Waldron made one of the greatest mistakes in his career. Instead of attempting to follow the limousine and ascertain Mme. Madcap's address, he shrugged his shoulders and turned away.

VIII

Brone Awakes

Sambo's face was inscrutable as he held open the door of the limousine for Mme. Madcap and her somewhat inebriated escort. Delighted at what he fondly thought was his capture of the masked beauty, Hamilton Brone had taken more wine while waiting for her to leave the café. He had not spoken to Wallace Melkington again, but he had met Waldron and had sneered in his face and boasted of his conquest. And he was aware that Waldron had seen him getting into the limousine.

Sambo got behind the wheel and started to drive uptown. Mme. Madcap watched through the rear window and made sure that they were not being followed; and then she picked up the speaking tube and gave Sambo an order which meant that he was to drive to the house far downtown.

Hamilton Brone did not notice when the

limousine turned, had not noticed in which direction it was going in the first place, and would not have cared had he known. He began an attempt at love-making and found that he was not succeeding.

"Wait, silly, until we are home!" Mme. Madcap said. "There are windows in the car, and we both have reputations—of a sort."

Brone sat in one corner of the seat, heavy with wine, his eyes half-closed and his breathing deep. He was drowsy because of the liquor he had taken and from the motion of the limousine. Since Mme. Madcap wished it, he would wait until they had reached her home before continuing with his love-making attempts.

Mme. Madcap watched him carefully from the corners of her eyes, realized his condition, and knew he was on the verge of a drunken slumber. Beneath the shelter of her cloak, she reached into the bosom of her gown and removed something that glittered in the light. It was a tiny hypodermic needle, charged and ready for use.

Again she looked at Hamilton Brone, and then bent forward and clasped one of his wrists. She spoke in a low tone, and he did not reply.

Brone merely muttered something that was unintelligible. He made an effort to rouse himself and failed. He imagined there was a quick sting in his wrist, and he moved it languidly.

Mme. Madcap gave a sigh of relief and put the hypodermic needle away. Hamilton Brone started to totter forward, and she thrust him back into the corner of the car. His head drooped; his form relaxed. Sambo drove on.

This time Sambo did not stop at the curb, but turned the big limousine into the alley and ran along it until the car was opposite the little door. Then he stopped the machine and sprang out. He glanced up and down the alley and then opened the door.

Mme. Madcap stepped out and unlocked the door of the house, and Sambo reached in and took the unconscious form of Hamilton Brone in his arms. He carried him through the narrow hallway while Mme. Madcap lit the path with her electric torch. Up the stairs they went, and to the prison room with its two cells. There was a couch in one corner of the room; Sambo stretched the form of the unconscious Hamilton Brone upon it.

"Put away the limousine, then hurry back," Mme. Madcap said. "You know what you have to do."

Some time later, Brone fought his ways back to consciousness. He realized that he was very weak, that he was bathed in perspiration, that he was stretched upon some sort of bed, and that it was dark.

He closed his eyes and tried to breathe regularly, tried to collect his scattered wits and reason things out.

Brone opened his eyes again—and again he faced the darkness. Not a ray of light came to his vision. He struggled to sit up and finally managed it. For a moment he held his head in his hands, and then he lifted it and tried to pierce the blackness that surrounded him. He reached for a handkerchief to wipe the perspiration from his face—and found that he had no hip pocket where one should have been.

He felt his clothing. This coarse coat he never had felt before, these baggy, stiff trousers—they had not come from his tailor. The shoes seemed to be made of lead.

He put one hand to his throbbing head—and almost screamed. His thick, curly hair—which often had endeared him to women—was gone. His head was shaved!

Hamilton Brone began to be alarmed. Often, after an excess of drinking, he had experience peculiar feelings, but nothing to compare with this. He felt the bed upon which he sat and discovered it was made of a blanket stretched on a meshwork of steel.

Brone staggered to his feet and took two quick steps forward to crash against steel bars. He recoiled, reached out his hands, grasped the bars, and shook them. He turned to the right, took three steps, and crashed against more bars. He faced about, staggered forward, and met steel bars again.

For an instant he was still, listening, unable to hear a sound save his own heavy breathing. The quiet, the darkness seemed to be smothering him. For a moment he endured it, and then he screamed!

He stumbled against the bed, crashed down upon it, sprang up and screamed again. He hurled himself against the bars that he could feel but could not see. He beat against them with his fists, pounded his head against them, shrieked like a soul in torment.

A door was thrown open; a shaft of light entered. Hamilton Brone could see the shadow of a man. And then there came a soft click, and light flooded him and the space about him. And a hoarse voice cried:

"At it again, are you? Stop that noise or I'll give you something to howl for! Think you can pull this stunt every night?"

Weak, trembling, Hamilton Brone sprang back a step and glared around him. He was in a cage—a cell. Adjoining it was another cell. Once more he sprang to the bars and looked at the man standing just outside. That man wore the uniform of a prison guard.

"What—what—" Hamilton Brone began gasping.

"You stop that noise, or I'll tell the warden and he'll 'tend to you!" the guard said.

Brone stared at him in amazement. He did not know that this was a masquerade, that the guard was "Red" Riley, gangster, burglar, all-around crook.

"Where—am I?" Brone asked.

"A lot of fool information you're wantin'." Riley told him. "If you don't know, and it'll do you any good to learn, I'll remark that you are in the State's prison, and that you've been here two weeks—and a devil of a two weeks it's been!"

"Prison? Two weeks?" Brone gasped. "I can't understand! Why? What for? I—I seem to remember leaving the café—with a woman—and that's all."

"You left the café with a woman, all right, according to the newspapers at the time," "Red" Riley told him. "But that was more than three months ago. It won't get you anything to try that loss-of-memory stuff on me. You should have handed that to the judge."

Hamilton Brone sat down weakly and looked up at the man on the other side of the bars.

"What—what does it mean?" he asked.

"Well, what is it that you can't remember?" Riley countered. "How much can you remember?"

"I—I was at the café—"

"Where you had the row with the Melkington man?"

"I—I told him to mind his business, I think—and told Lionel Waldron the same. I remember now! That masked woman—Mme. Madcap! I left the café with her. We got into her limousine."

"Quite a little memory you have," Riley sneered. "Suppose you tell the story yourself."

"But there my memory stops. I—I can't understand—"

"You was full of wine, wasn't you? Yes! You started off in the limousine with that woman, old top, and you ran amuck before it had gone three blocks. You tried to strangle Mme. Madcap, and she yelled and the chauffeur stopped the car—"

"I didn't!"

"Shut up! I'm telling this story. I should think you'd want to forget it. The chauffeur stopped the car, I said, and tried to help her. You smashed him in the jaw and took off on the fly—a mob at your heels.

You dodged 'em and went back to the café and walked in like you was as sober as a judge—some judges, that is."

"I—I don't remember any of it—"

"Shut up! You walked into that café and found this Melkington man sittin' at a table with a couple of women. You sat down at another table and ordered a bottle of wine. Remember that? No? Well, you drank the wine, according to the testimony, and then you picked up the bottle, walked over to that other table, and smashed this Melkington man across the head with it, cracking his skull neatly."

"I—I did that? I didn't—"

"Shut up! You did, and you know it. About three hundred people, more or less, saw you. There was some muss—women shriekin' and men runnin' around and all that. A nice time was had by all. You smashed half a dozen waiters before they got you down and sat on you and hauled you away to the cooler—"

Hamilton Brone, gasping, sprang to his feet.

"Go on! What else?"

"Well, they hauled you to jail, as you know very well, and all the time you kept howlin' that you'd busted Melkington's head, and that you'd bust the head of anybody else who tried to cut you out with this Mme. Madcap person. That night, Melkington slipped his cable."

"Dead? Wallace Melkington dead?"

"And buried more than three months ago, you simp!" Riley told him. "That made it a murder charge, of course. And you hopped into court and said you'd done it and would do it again if the judge would turn you loose and give you a chance. So we got you. And a sweet time we've had of it. You've been a ravin' fool ever since you've been here—had to be put in this room in solitary—and if anybody asks me, I'd say you're making a play to get sent to the insane asylum and afterward released—and that it ain't going to work!"

Brone clutched at the bars, his eyes bulging, his breath coming in quick gasps, a great fear in his heart.

"I—I was found guilty of murder?" he asked.

"You admitted it—as you know very well. There were almost a hundred witnesses—and you know that. And you raved about that Mme. Madcap person so much that your own wife didn't even go to jail to see you."

"She—deserted me?"

"She was in a sanitarium, her nerves frazzled," Riley said. "You played hob generally. Why a man with oodles of coin will run amuck and raise hades is more than I can say. With all your coin you could have had a hot time all your life. But you had to hit the booze and get mixed up with bum women—"

"It can't be true!" Brone cried. "I don't remember any of it!"

"Well, you're here, aren't you? Isn't that the answer? Don't try any of your funny stuff on me! Give it to the prison doctor— I'm fed up on it."

"And I'm—in prison?" Brone gasped. He looked at the bars again, looked at the other little cell.

"You certainly are in prison," Riley answered.

"For—for how—long?"

Hamilton Brone licked his dry lips and waited for the reply.

"From now on!" "Red" Riley said. "Forever. For life! Until death do us part!"

IX

A Family Gathering

To reach the domicile of "Shifty" Slade, one went down a certain alley that was pitch dark at night, cluttered with tin cans and odds and ends of building material, and permeated with an odor offensive to delicate nostrils.

At a certain place, one came to a rickety door that swung on creaking hinges. The door opened, a person found himself confronted by a narrow, dark hallway, at the end of which was a flight of stairs that seldom were swept and never repaired. Slade had a room at the top of the rickety stairs, and the room held nothing more than a faded rug, a washstand and a table and two chairs.

It was one o'clock that night when "Shifty" Slade turned out the gas and got into bed.

It was a quarter past two o'clock when "Shifty" Slade awoke, his eyes bulging, the lids blinking rapidly in the glare of a flashlight.

"Shifty" Slade sat up quickly on the side of the bed. All he could see was a circle of flame, and in one edge of it the muzzle of an automatic that menaced him.

"Light your gas, man!" a voice from the dark commanded. "And don't try to do anything else if you have any ambitions to see the sun rise and hear the birds sing in the morning."

"Shifty" Slade, now thoroughly awake, stood up and went to the foot of his bed. He reached into his coat pocket and took out a small box of matches. He went on to the wall gas-jet and struck one of the matches against it. He turned on the gas and applied the flaming match. The room was filled with a sudden yellow glare.

"Shifty" Slade turned around slowly. He saw a gigantic black man standing within eight feet of him, grinning, showing two rows of even white teeth.

"Well, what's the idea?" Slade wanted to know. "How'd you get in here? Who are you? What do you want?"

"Get on your shirt and pants, man. A lady is going to visit you in about two minutes, and you ain't properly dressed," the black man told him, menacing him with the revolver. Slade's weapon was hidden in a drawer of the washstand, which was on the opposite side of the room, and he could do nothing but obey.

Slade dressed rapidly and sat down on the side of the bed again. The black man, still watching him, stepped backward to the door and tapped upon it. It opened instantly.

Slade rubbed at his eyes again. Before him stood a woman in a long, black cloak. Over her face was a black mask that fitted tightly, and the hood of her cloak covered her head. The cloak parted in front and "Shifty" Slade saw a gorgeous evening gown beneath it.

"I want you!" the woman said.

"I don't get this," Slade stammered.

"I have work for you to do," the woman went on. "You are one of the men selected. I have come for you, rather than send for you, because I want no mistakes made, and there is no time to lose."

"But—who are you?"

"I am known as Mme. Madcap."

"Oh!" Slade exclaimed. "You're the dame that's been settin' them crazy uptown, are you? I've been hearin' a lot about you lately. What's the lay?"

"I have picked you for my organization. I always pick the best men, specialists, artist in their lines. There will be greater profit than you ever have known. All you have to do is obey orders."

"What do you want me to do?"

"Come with me to my headquarters, take orders from me—and your share of the profits," she said. "I assure you that you'll be satisfied."

"And work in the same crowd as "Red" Riley? Not if I know myself!"

Mme. Madcap stepped closer to him and spoke in a lower tone.

"I am used to having my orders obeyed," she

said. "You'll do as I say, or you can go to jail for a twenty-stretch."

"Don't make me laugh."

"I can tip off the police in fifteen minutes to things that would send you up for life," she said.

"Bunk!"

"How about that little matter last summer—the jewels that were taken from the deposit box of a certain famous actress?" she asked. "I know that the cops went wild on that, but I can put them on the right trail in five minutes. How about the night you slipped away by yourself and hit a young millionaire a little too hard with your blackjack? You took matters into your own hands that night, didn't you? Bill Duncan did not send you on that job."

"Who—what do you mean?" Slade gasped.

"You know what I mean! You do as I say, or you'll be on your way up the river with forty-eight hours. Are you a fool? I'm offering you a connection with the cleverest gang that ever existed in this old town, a chance to line your pocketbook, and you're trying to turn it down."

"But what's the lay?" Slade persisted.

"You'll know that later. There will be plenty of action and money—and plenty of glory. Within a week, you'll be proud of the fact that you belong to Mme. Madcap's gang."

She reached in the bosom of her gown and took out a billfold. "Shifty" Slade gasped when he saw its contents. He gasped again when Mme. Madcap took out two one-hundred dollar bills and tossed them on the bed beside him.

"Just to bind the bargain," she said.

The following morning, acting under orders of Mme. Madcap, "Red" Riley set forth to find "Gentleman Joe" Marget. He located him within the hour.

"Well, I spoke to Mme. Madcap about you," he said, "and she wants to talk to you. Come along with me."

He took Marget to the house and up the stairs to the parlor on the second floor. Mme. Madcap, masked, was sitting at the end of the long table. Her eyes glittered as she looked at the man before her.

"So you are 'Gentleman Joe' Marget, are you?" she asked. "And you wish to become associated with me."

"That's what I told Riley," Marget said.

"I demand absolute loyalty," she told Marget. "You understand what that means?"

"I never doublecross my pals," Marget said.

"It wouldn't pay in this case!" Mme. Madcap told him, her voice hard for an instant. "Very well—we'll try you. You'll be given a room upstairs and you have nothing to do but await orders. Do not leave the house today or tomorrow without permission. We have something to do tomorrow night, and it will prove profitable. Do you understand?"

"I guess that's plain enough," Marget said.

"At the front of the hall upstairs you will find a sort of lounging-room, where you may talk with the others, or smoke or play cards. You'll find 'Shifty' Slade there now."

Riley led Marget away, showed him his room, and then directed him to the room where Slade was playing solitaire. Slade looked up and grinned as he entered.

"So she landed you, too, did she?" Slade asked. "What do you think of this stunt?"

"It looks good to me," Marget confessed.

"Well, we'll stick around long enough to see what happens," Slade said, lowering his voice. "But don't forget that you belong to the Slade gang."

"What do you mean by that?" Marget said.

"We may be able to find out a few things, and then sort of take charge ourselves," Slade whispered.

The door opened again, and Sambo ushered in Brute Wilger himself. And then Sambo was thrust aside, and the professor entered the room.

"Ah! Quite a family gathering," he said. "I understand that all you gentlemen are—er—members of the same club. Or is it a gang? No matter."

Slade and Marget were upon their feet and against the wall, hatred flaming in their faces.

"Belligerent, eh?" the professor asked. "Under existing circumstances, I deem it better for you to forego animosity toward me. We are to work together, in a way, for common profit. It is true that you gentlemen do not belong to the same organization as Mr. 'Red' Riley, for instance, but what of that? Mme. Madcap has gathered the best men and surely rival chieftains may bury the hatchet for a time—especially if there is big money in it."

"Money talks with me," said Marget.

"I understand that Mme. Madcap has issued orders that you gentlemen, who are close friends, shall have this little lounging-room for yourselves. Mr. Riley and others you do not like personally will have other quarters. Mme. Madcap now has a housekeeper and a cook, and meals will be served you here. You need not associate with Mr. Riley, nor with me, except during—er—business hours."

With that the professor disappeared and Sambo went out and closed the door.

X

The Robbery

At four o'clock that afternoon, Sambo entered the lounging-room where Slade, Marget and Wilger were playing cards and announced that their presence was desired by Mme. Madcap in the parlor on the floor below. They tossed the cards aside and followed Sambo through the hall, down the stairs, and to the parlor where Mme. Madcap sat at one end of the long table waiting for them. "Red" Riley and the professor were sitting near her.

"The time has come for business," Mme. Madcap said. "Tonight, we shall enter and loot the residence of Miss Dorcas Darcan. It is just off Fifth Avenue. I'll give you the address later. When I undertake a thing, I ascertain all facts that may help me. So-called criminals would make fewer mistakes and suffer less incarceration if they would do the same. Knowledge is an excellent thing. Always know all about your prospective victim, and then you will not be surprised and caught because some minor detail was overlooked.

"Miss Dorcas Darcan is a rich orphan. She has been educated abroad. Her father left her a large fortune, and she purchased the splendid house we are going to visit tonight and made her home there.

"Before we start, I shall give you a plan of the house and outline the course we are to follow in taking care of the servants and securing the loot. I will take command and give such further orders as may become necessary.

"There is a safe in the library. In the safe there will be some money, of course, as a sum is kept there for current expenses. There will be some negotiable bonds, too. I intend to get a string of pearls from Miss Darcan; I know where she keeps them in her boudoir, and they are said to be worth about $20,000. I expect this haul to net $30,000 at least. Go back now, play cards, eat dinner, and wait for me to send for you."

Commencing at ten o'clock that evening, Mme. Madcap called for them one at a time, issued final instructions, and sent them on their way.

At one o'clock, Mme. Madcap was at the rendezvous and the limousine was in the alley, its lights extinguished. The others of the band were crouching in the darkness against the alley wall.

They went inside and found themselves in a small garden. Mme. Madcap called Slade and Brute Wilger to her.

"There is the garage," she said. "Here is a duplicate key to the side door. Enter that way, pass through to the chauffeur's room, and make sure that he is bound and gagged. Use no more violence than is necessary."

From the limousine, Sambo had taken small, stout ropes and materials for gags, and he supplied the men. In a few minutes they returned from the chauffeur's room, their work accomplished.

Mme. Madcap took out another key and unlocked the door, and they slipped into the house and made their way toward the servants' quarters.

"The butler's room!" Mme. Madcap whispered, pointing to the door. "Professor, you and Mr. Riley have work to do there."

The professor and "Red" Riley stepped aside and up to the door, and Mme. Madcap led Slade and Wilger on down the hall. "Gentleman Joe" Marget was watching outside, in front; Sambo was in the alley near the limousine.

"Now for the other servants," Mme. Madcap said. "The housekeeper, the cook and two maids—all women. The two maids use that room, the cook and the housekeeper the one opposite. Undoubtedly they are in bed and asleep. Wait here, and I'll handle them myself."

Slade and Wilger waited. Mme. Madcap unlocked the door to the right and slipped inside, closing the door after her again. When she returned, she had a towel in her hand, a bottle in the other.

"It was not difficult," she said. "I used chloroform. Now I'll lock them in."

She did so, leaving the key in the lock, and then crossed the hall to the other door, opened it, and disappeared. She was back soon, with the announcement that the two maids had been chloroformed, too; and she locked that door and left the key in the lock.

There was a commotion in the butler's room, but Mme. Madcap restrained Slade and Wilger from entering. The professor and Riley should be able to take care of things there, she said, and a few minutes later the professor joined them in the hall; "Red" Riley remaining to guard the butler, as he had been instructed.

"There is the dining room," Mme. Madcap explained. "You'll find an excellent silver service there. When you have finished, go to the library, that room at the end of the hall. Take anything of value you find, but do not touch the safe; we don't want fingerprints. I'll pay a visit to Miss Dorcas Darcan myself."

Slade and Wilger slipped into the dining room and began their work, the professor following them and aiding in putting the silver in bags they had carried for the purpose. Busy searching for valuables, they gave no attention to Mme. Madcap's part of the enterprise. Once they heard a woman scream, and presently Mme. Madcap came down the stairs to them.

"Well, I got the pearls," she said, "and I was forced to put Miss Dorcas Darcan to sleep. Now to finish and get out. Professor, call Mr. Riley here."

The professor hurried away on his mission, and

Mme. Madcap went into the library. Wilger and Slade had found only a few articles of value.

Riley came to the library, and Mme. Madcap held the torch and played the light on the door of the safe. Riley was prepared for the task. He drew on thin rubber gloves that would prevent fingerprints, knelt before the strongbox, and began cracking the combination.

For five minutes he worked, now and then grunting in disgust, and then he gave voice to a whistle. Victory! He stood up and threw the door of the safe open. Mme. Madcap played the light inside. Riley ripped open the strongbox and took out some currency, which he handed up to Mme. Madcap. A couple of diamond rings followed, and an old-fashioned bracelet.

He investigated another compartment and found a few bonds. Then he went through the safe methodically, handing things to Mme. Madcap, who discarded most of them as worthless or unsalable.

"That's all!" "Red" Riley said.

"Leave the door open and step back," Mme. Madcap commanded.

Riley saw that she had a package in her hand; and now she opened it and took out a rubber glove. She handled it carefully, drew it on her hand cautiously, and pressed the tips of her fingers against the polished door of the safe, near the combination knob.

"What's the idea?" Riley wanted to know.

"To throw the police off the track—and on a certain other track," she whispered in reply. "I got a cake of soap Hamilton Brone used yesterday when you let him wash his face and hands. His fingerprints were upon it. I prepared this rubber glove with a coating that took up the fingerprints from the soap—"

"And you've just transferred this Brone's fingerprints to the safe door?" Riley gasped.

"Exactly!"

"I getcha! The cops know Brone has disappeared, they know he was crazy about you, and went away from the café with you and hasn't been seen since—"

"Precisely," Mme. Madcap interrupted. "And if they find that these fingerprints are Hamilton Brone's, they will think that he was so infatuated with me that he's turned crook to help me steal. Come, now, our work is finished."

They gathered in the hall, and Mme. Madcap led them toward the rear door.

"Go out one at a time and scatter," she directed. "Get home as quickly as possible. Professor, you'll be the last to leave, before me."

One by one, they slipped through the door and into the darkness, each man to use his own skill in getting from the dangerous neighborhood and back downtown. Slade was told to inform Marget, watching the front, that he was free to make his getaway. The professor and Mme. Madcap were the last to leave the house.

XI

Waldron Takes the Trail

On the second morning after Hamilton Brone left the café in company with Mme. Madcap, Lionel Waldron was awakened by his manservant at six o'clock.

"Telephone, sir," the man said. "I did my best to say that you could not possibly answer before ten o'clock, sir, knowing that you had retired thoroughly exhausted, but the party insisted that I call you. Very important, they said—a lady, sir."

"Give her name?"

"Mrs. Hamilton Brone, sir."

Waldron sprang from bed, put on dressing gown and slippers, and stepped into the next room, where there was an extension of the telephone.

"Hello!" he cried into the transmitter.

"Lionel? This is Elizabeth Brone. Pardon me for calling you at such an early hour, but I felt that I should. Can you come over right away?"

"Certainly," Waldron said. "Is there anything wrong?"

"It's about—about Hamilton," Elizabeth Brone said. "Please come to me at once."

Waldron dressed as quickly as possible, bolted a piece of toast, gulped some coffee, and hurried down to his waiting car.

Waldron's chauffeur lost no time in getting to the address and Waldron found himself admitted instantly, and conducted to the library. A glance at Elizabeth Brone told him that she had not retired the night before. There was fear in her face, and she had been weeping.

"What is it, Elizabeth?" Waldron asked.

"It is Hamilton," she replied. "He has not been home for three nights. He has been infatuated with some masked woman who has been seen around the cafés. They call her Mme. Madcap. Some of my friends have told me, Lionel. Oh, I assure you I have no pride remaining! Three nights ago, he left the café with that woman—and he had not been seen since. Nor has this Mme. Madcap."

"What?" Waldron gasped. The last was news to him.

"I want you to find him, Lionel," Elizabeth Brone said. "He may be in trouble—may be detained by fore. That creature may have accomplices, and they may be trying to get money from him. Please do your best, Lionel. I have a feeling of fear. If it is money, help him to buy himself out and let us have as little scandal as possible. I know Hamilton Brone is not worthy of my respect, but I have not ceased to love him. And I keep telling myself that he will settle down one day."

"I'll do my best," Waldron said.

He was very thoughtful as he left the Brone residence and drove slowly downtown. He visited the café and had a talk with the manager, visited several clubs where Hamilton Brone held membership, and found no trace of the man. At nine o'clock the following morning, while waiting for his toast and coffee, Waldron opened the first morning paper that came to his hand and began glancing at the headlines. An article on the front page attracted him.

He sat forward in his chair, astonishment written on his face as he read. He saw that the paper was a late morning edition. It told of the robbery of the residence of Miss Dorcas Darcan, a wealthy orphan who recently had purchased property and made a home in the city. A valuable string of pearls had been taken, silverware had been stolen, the library safe had been opened and jewels and bonds removed.

The robbery in itself was worth the story the newspaper gave it, but the astounding part for Waldron was the statement of Miss Darcan that a woman had robbed her. She had been awakened by the light, she said, and found a masked woman in her room. She had attempted to fight, but had been overpowered. The woman said that she was Mme. Madcap, and then had chloroformed her victim.

Servants had told the police that there were several men associated with the masked woman. The chauffeur had been bound and gagged in the garage by two men. Jordan, the butler, had been overpowered and rendered helpless.

"A crook!" Waldron gasped. "She's a crook!"

This rather complicated the Brone affair. Surely Brone was not implicated in a robbery.

"I've got to get that Mme. Madcap to find out about Brone," he told himself. "And the police will be after her, too, after this."

He rushed for his bath, determined to dress as quickly as possible and take up the trail. But before he could leave the apartment, he had a caller, a man from police headquarters.

Waldron knew the man, a shrewd detective named Macguire. And he knew that Macguire had not visited him at that hour of the morning merely to pass the time of day. Macguire did not leave him long in doubt concerning the object of his visit.

"Read about the Darcan robbery?" he asked.

"Just a few minutes ago," Waldron replied.

"What do you know about this Mme. Madcap person?"

"I saw her at the café several times," Waldron answered. "I know that Hamilton Brone and Wallace Melkington were crazy about the woman. I suppose you know that Brone has been missing several days. I thought at first that he was with that woman, carrying on an affair. Now I don't know what to think."

"He was pretty well infatuated with that woman, wasn't he?" Macguire asked.

"He appeared to be, but Brone got infatuated with some woman every six months."

"I guess there is no doubt that she is a clever crook and probably the head of a gang. We might as well come to the point. A few years ago, you started out to study fingerprints in connection with your business, didn't you?"

"Yes, and now I have an important collection."

"And early in the game you took prints of a lot of your friends?"

"Yes; but what has that got to do with this case?"

"Got a card with Brone's fingerprints?"

"I believe I have."

"Please let me see it," said Macguire.

Wondering what was coming, Waldron went to his file cases in another room and returned with the card. Macguire inspected the prints through a magnifying glass.

"Hum!" he said. "Waldron, here is something funny. We found fingerprints on the front of the safe at the Darcan place. And they are the fingerprints of Hamilton Brone—as I can tell from this card."

"Why, that's impossible!" Waldron cried.

"Fingerprints do not lie, Waldron, and you know it! And Hamilton Brone is not known personally to Miss Darcan and has never been in her house to her knowledge, so he never touched the safe innocently. Know what it means? That Brone is so infatuated with this Mme. Madcap that he has turned crook to please her."

"Nonsense!" Waldron cried; but he was half afraid it was the truth.

"We got a note this morning by special messenger that puts us on the track. The messenger said an ordinary-appearing man gave it to him on the street, said he was a detective and paid him well to carry it to us. Here is the note, Waldron."

Waldron unfolded it and read:

If, in investigating the Darcan house robbery, you find fingerprints on the safe, and are unable to find duplicates in your files, go to Lionel Waldron, look through his private files, and ask particularly to see the fingerprints of Hamilton Brone.

Waldron handed the note back.

"You see?" said Macguire.

"It isn't possible."

"Anything is possible when a man goes crazy over a woman," the headquarters' man declared.

"But who would send that note?"

"Why not some member of this Mme. Madcap's gang, say some man Brone had displaced in her affections. It has happened a few thousand times before. Well, thanks for your help, Waldron."

Macguire hurried away, and for an hour Waldron paced the floor and considered the case. He scarcely could bring himself to think that Brone had fallen so low, yet everything seemed to indicate it. And he did not know which way to turn. The police dragnet would be put in operation, of course, but something seemed to tell Lionel Waldron that Mme. Madcap would be clever enough to evade it.

XII

A Deal on the Side

At noon the following day, Mme. Madcap called the men together and handed each two hundred dollars.

"Some of the bonds we got at the Darcan house have been sold already," she explained. "The pearls are being handled by a fence I can trust. It will take some time to get the money, but we'll get more by not hurrying."

Late that afternoon, she summoned the professor to the parlor.

"All the boys in?" she asked.

"They never miss a meal, my dear Mme. Madcap," he said.

"Very well," she replied. "I want to see Marget here— alone. Find him and send him to me without the others knowing, if you can."

The professor hurried away, and soon Marget

entered the parlor. "Gentleman Joe" Marget's curiosity was aroused. He sat down at one end of the table and looked at her expectantly.

"Marget," Mme. Madcap said, "it is no more than natural that, when there are several men together, one or two may be superior to the others. As I have intimated, I have more than one iron in the fire at the same time. I am working to get results as speedily as possible. And I am judging you men rapidly."

Marget smiled at her; he took her words to mean that he was ahead of the others in some regard.

"Could you work alone—that is, without the other boys," madam asked.

Marget grinned at her.

"I'm on!" he said.

"Do you know the National Apartments?" she asked.

"I've passed the building and know that a lot of bachelors live there. Had my eye on it once, but never worked the game."

"That is the building in which we are interested," Mme. Madcap told him. "One of the wealthy bachelors is named Rufus Throckton. He is about fifty and very eccentric—I suppose most people would call him a freak. He is worth all kinds of money. Marget, this job is so easy and profitable that it sounds too good to be true."

"Well, what's the lay?"

"Rufus Throckton has a big living room and library combined. I'll give you a map of it, so you'll know where every chair is placed. In one corner, there is a safe. It is an old one, and generally is unlocked. There is also a desk in the room—a big desk that has four drawers, none of them locked. What would you say, Marget, if I told you that Rufus Throckton keeps in one of those unlocked drawers—and keeps it there all the time—a string of matched pearls worth about $10,000?"

"I'd say that either you were crazy to believe such a thing, or else he is crazy to do it."

"Well, he does it, Marget—and because he is crazy. Years ago—when Rufus Throckton was about twenty-five—he fell in love with a certain society girl. She was very beautiful and finally agreed to marry Throckton, most people said because of his wealth and not because she loved him. He was crazy about her, Marget. He bought that string of pearls for a wedding gift, thinking how they would look against her pretty throat."

"Simp!" "Gentleman Joe" Marget commented.

"And the night before the marriage, she ran away with the man she really loved, married him, and went to another section of the country to live," Mme. Madcap continued. "It almost killed Rufus Throckton. He went on a trip around the world, trying to forget. But he couldn't. And he always remained a bachelor. And he was crazy about that string of pearls. He kept them near him all the time."

"Simp."

"Marget, he keeps them now in an unlocked drawer of his desk. His valet is an honest man, and nobody else is supposed to know that the pearls are there. They are in the lower left-hand drawer, in a long case.

"That is the information I have, Marget, and I know that it is correct. And here is a sketch that shows how the rooms are arranged. His apartment is on the second floor, front, west side of the building. Right here is a little balcony, and at night it is absolutely dark, for the street lights do not touch it, and if there is a moon the building adjoining cuts off all light from the little court."

"I suppose we'll have to turn the trick late at night when everybody is asleep."

"Marget! What has become of your brains? That is exactly what an ordinary burglar would do. And the men who live in that building are leaving and entertaining at all hours of the night. The place never is altogether quiet. Some of them sit around their rooms and smoke and read until the small hours of the morning, and others are young fellows who like the bright lights and generally come home with the milkman."

"Well, then—"

"It must be done early in the evening, between eight and nine o'clock," she said.

"I can't see that the chances would be any better then," Marget replied. "Hasn't Throckton a valet?"

"He has, but you needn't worry about the servant. I'll attend to all that part of the work. All you have to do is be ready to rob the safe and get those pearls from the desk when I give the word. I'll know when Throckton dines out and when the valet is gone, too."

"How can we figure that?"

"I'll know, Marget; we'll not have to guess at it. And I'm pretty sure that it'll be tomorrow night. And now that you are going to work with me, there is another thing. If disaster ever comes, Marget, if you ever are nabbed, just sit tight and say nothing. A lawyer will be sent to you, and you'll enter a plea of not guilty and get admitted to bail. In a couple of weeks, after things have quieted down, bail will be supplied. And then you can simply beat it—jump bail, understand? I take care of my people."

"Well, that's a decent arrangement."

"I mean to tell the other boys that, too. The man who is caught, and who sits still and says nothing, will be cared for well. Not a word on the Throckton business to any of the others, Marget. This is just between ourselves. If you do this work right, there'll be some more special assignments—with big profits. That's all—you'd better go back to the other boys."

It was late in the afternoon of the following day when Mme. Madcap slipped into the narrow passage and went through it to the alley door. She removed her mask, put on a hat, unlocked the door and went out. Within a few minutes she was several blocks away and safe.

Once more she entered the subway and took a train for uptown. She journeyed to Grand Central Terminal and went into one of the public telephone booths. The number she called was that of police headquarters, and she asked for the captain of detectives who was an acknowledged leader in his line.

"Please pay close attention, captain," she said. "I shall tell you this once, and not repeat it, and shall refuse to answer any questions."

"What is it? Who is this?"

"My name does not matter at present. Pay attention!" Mme. Madcap said. "You caught William Duncan a few months ago, didn't you?"

"We certainly though so, and we think so yet."

"Would you like to get your hands on the members of the old Duncan gang, catch them where they would surely be convicted?"

"Certainly!"

"Very well, captain! I'm going to turn the old Duncan gang over to you—one at a time. There is no special reason just now, except that I wish to do it. And you can have the first man tonight. Know Rufus Throckton and where he lives?"

"Yes."

"Know 'Gentleman Joe' Marget?"

"I certainly do."

"He is one of the old Duncan gang, but you haven't a thing on him, and you know it. But you can get something on him tonight. At 8:30, Marget is going to ransack Rufus Throckton's apartment. I happen to know it. He'll enter from the little balcony that is in the dark. Throckton will be to dinner, and his valet will be lured away. Isn't that all it is necessary for me to tell you?"

"Thanks," the captain said. "Maybe it's a joke, but I'll investigate it. But—who are you?"

"I told you that I'd answer no questions," she said. "If you do your work well tonight maybe I'll do you another favor in a day or two."

Mme. Madcap hung up the receiver and walked from the booth. She was smiling when she caught a downtown express. She gained the alley, opened the door, hung up her hat and put on her mask, and went on into the house.

XIII

Love Stuff

"Shifty" Slade looked up as Brute Wilger entered the lounging-room, and put aside the deck of cards with which he had been playing solitaire. Wilger dropped into a chair and touched a match to a cigarette.

"Seen Marget?" Slade asked.

"Not since late yesterday afternoon."

"Neither have I," Slade said. "He ducked out of here early last night, and he hasn't shown up this morning, and I took the trouble to find out that his bed hasn't been slept in. What's the answer?"

"Search me," Wilger said.

The door was thrown open, and the grinning Sambo entered.

"Mme. Madcap wants you all to come down to the parlor," he said. "She has some information to impart."

They followed Sambo down the stairs and walked into the room. Mme. Madcap, masked, sat at her usual place at the head of the table, and on one side of it were "Red" Riley and the professor. Marget was not there.

Mme. Madcap's first sentence startled them.

"'Gentleman Joe' Marget is in jail!" she said.

"What's that?" Slade cried, bending forward, an expression of amazement in his face.

"I have ascertained that he was arrested last night a little before nine o'clock. He was caught robbing an apartment far uptown, caught in the act. 'Gentleman Joe' Marget, it seems, found my methods too slow for him and decided to go it alone for once. You know the result."

"Why, the poor boob! He never did have sense enough to work alone, unless it was swindlin' a hick!" "Shifty" Slade declared. "I always was a bit suspicious of that bird. I've watched him at times. So they got him, did they?"

"And I called all of you here for this conference to decide what is to be done about it," Mme. Madcap said. "He really was a member of your gang, Slade, as I understand it. I told you that, if disaster comes, all you had to do was to sit tight, and you'd be released on bail in a short time. But this thing is just a bit different. If he had been caught while helping to carry out one of our plans—"

"The big boob!" Slade interrupted.

"It is for you men to decide. Shall we bail him out, let him make his getaway, and forfeit the bail money? Or shall we simply let him handle his own affairs? He will have a big share coming from the Darcan job as soon as the fence reports to me. If we stand by him, he gets it. If we decide to punish him by letting him drift, his share will be divided among you. I have determined to let you men decide it."

"Shifty" Slade licked at his lips. "Red" Riley and the professor had no hand in this, nor did Brute Wilger. Marget has been Slade's man, and it was for Slade to decide his fate.

"Let him get out of the best way he can!" Slade decided, finally. "Maybe it'll be a lesson for him. A man like that would be liable to double-cross his pals."

That seemed to settle it. Mme. Madcap announced that she agreed with the decision, and the men left the parlor—all but the professor, whom Mme. Madcap had privately signaled to remain. She bade him be seated again.

"It is dirty work!" Mme. Madcap declared. "To be surrounded by persons you cannot trust is not a nice experience. But, in a business like this, it is necessary at times."

"That is to be deplored," the professor said.

"You are one man I feel that I can trust," she said.

"I thank you for you confidence."

"I have had you investigated," she admitted. "I did not believe your story at first—not all of it. But I know now that you are deliberately throwing away an honorable career to begin a life of crime."

"The advantages—the monetary gain—"

"Listen to me, Prof. Salwick! I know of what I am speaking, too. It is advantage at first, and then it degenerates into a sordid sort of intermittent excitement. About the only real sensation a criminal knows after a time is that of fear. And it is a sensation of real fear."

"I—er—I suppose so," the professor said.

"You cannot begin to comprehend it," Mme. Madcap continued. "It is a terrible thing. Every minute you expect an officer to touch you on the shoulder. Every minute you have a vision of cold stone walls, harsh prison guards, coarse food and clothing. You have the dread of becoming a mere thing, your every move marked out by another man, of losing your identity, trading your name for a number, incurring the stigma the nothing can remove."

"What a dismal picture!" he said.

"I am not jesting, professor. The general public little knows what the professional criminal endures. And the women? Have you ever stopped to think, professor, what it might mean to the wives and daughters of professional criminals?"

"I must confess that I have not."

"Their men go out to fight society as warriors to fight a foe. And like the wives and daughters of warriors, the criminal's women wait at home, fearing for news, wondering what is transpiring—where he is now, whether he is in danger. And they welcome his return as warrior's women welcome his return from the wars. But they do not have the uplifting feeling of glory, of excellent work well done, that the warrior's women have. If he fails—and fails—they do not have the knowledge that he did well—they have only shame."

"What a graphic picture!" the professor said. "But why speak of dismal things?"

"I am trying to show you the truth," said Mme. Madcap. "I am showing you the reality of the criminal's life. The glamour soon wears away, and there is nothing left but endless misery."

"Really, I am feeling distressed," declared the professor. "And why do you tell me these things?"

"Because it is not too late for you to turn back. This is but an adventure for you, Prof. Salwick. I have been with you considerably, and perhaps I have studied you a bit, in the days when you escorted me to the café, and since. Pardon me, but you do not have the criminal spirit. You'll never be a successful criminal. Believe me, I know. Your feelings, your ethics are too fine."

"Why, I am surprised! I had thought that I was getting along famously."

"Oh, you have so far—but you have scarcely begun," she replied. "You have been indulging in child's play so far. You are implicated with me now, of course, yet there may be some way out. And think what wonderful work you can do in your own field!"

"Well, there is—er—another reason why I desire to continue with the work," the professor said. "I would be in your environment—be on the same social plane."

"I beg your pardon?"

"I presume that this is rather unexpected, my dear, but I have grown to have a certain feeling for you. It is rather a peculiar thing, for I have seldom given thought to women. There is something about you, it appears, that rather intoxicates me, if I may use the term."

"Why, professor, I do not understand."

"Your nearness is bewitching," he continued. "I dare not hope to win you, yet it is a great deal to be near you—"

"Prof. Salwick! Are you trying to say that you—you admire me?"

"Admire," said the professor, "is one of those useless words that have neither strength nor weakness, if you can gather my meaning. I—that is, I love you!"

He made his avowal in a matter-of-fact manner, but his heart was pounding at his ribs, and Mme. Madcap guessed it from the expression on his face.

"You love me?" she said softly. "And you know me as a criminal, yet you love me?"

"I do not care what is your status among the narrow-minded of the Earth, of whom there are a great many," said Prof. Salwick. "It is true that I know you only as Mme. Madcap. I do not care whether your genuine name is Gertie or Gwendolyn. Is it either? No matter! I have ascertained that love is a peculiar thing. As I have said, I cannot hope to win you. I am not the romantic type. I cannot fancy myself playing a guitar beneath a window, for instance."

"I should hope not!" said Mme. Madcap.

"But I know my feelings and can trust them," he went on. "Without a doubt, I love you. And so, please, let me be near you. I realize that I am worthless, in a way—"

"You are not!" she exclaimed. "You are a splendid man! You have bodily strength—you have brains. Must I defend you against yourself?"

"I mean that I am almost worthless as a criminal."

"Thank heaven!" she said. "And let us say no more about this now, please. But I am honest enough to tell you this—I admire you a great deal."

"I thank you!" said Prof. Salwick.

XIV

The Betrayal

After breakfast the following morning, Mme. Madcap slipped through the passage and out of the building.

She walked down the street for half a dozen blocks and went into a telephone booth. Once more she called police headquarters and got the captain of detectives on the wire.

"Well, I see that you got 'Gentleman Joe' Marget," she said.

"Are you the woman who tipped that off?" the captain asked.

"I am."

"Well, whoever you are, I want to thank you for it. You certainly gave me the correct dope. 'Gentleman Joe' hasn't said a word since his arrest, but he seems to be getting mighty nervous about something. I don't suppose you care to tell me your name?"

"I don't mind. I am Mme. Madcap."

"What's that?" the captain shrieked into the transmitter.

"I told you the truth—I am Mme. Madcap," she replied. "And don't get all fussed up about it and have visions of catching me, for you can't do it. Better land the members of the old Duncan gang first, hadn't you? Are you ready for another of them?"

"I certainly am," the captain said.

"Just forget Mme. Madcap for a time, and you'll land more than one," she continued. "Do you happen to know a man called Brute Wilger?"

"I do. Did he belong to the old Duncan gang?"

"He did," said Mme. Madcap. "And you haven't a thing on him now, as you know very well. You can't get him for his past crimes, but you can get something on him this afternoon. And be sure that you get plenty of witnesses."

"I'll attend to that, all right!"

"I want you to be at a certain little café this afternoon about five o'clock. I'll give you the address just before I hang up. Get your eye on Wilger and watch him closely without being seen. Just grab him the moment you have something on him—that's all."

"You can bet I'll do that!"

"And, if you do it right, I'll hand over another man soon."

She gave him the address of the café, hung up the receiver, and hurried back down the street. Safe in the narrow passage once more, she put on her mask and went back to the parlor. "Red" Riley and the professor were playing cards.

"You two may go out this afternoon and get some fresh air," she said. "Be careful, of course. And please leave me now. Professor, find Sambo in the upper hall and tell him to send Mr. Wilger to me here."

She did not have to wait long. Within three minutes, Brute Wilger entered the parlor, closed the door at her command, and then sat down at one end of the long table. Mme. Madcap regarded him carefully for a moment.

"I wonder how far I can trust you?" she said.

"To the limit," Wilger declared.

"Do you think I'll be safe in trusting you on a delicate mission?"

"You know it!"

"Very well. I am going to trust you. I want you to be at a certain place this afternoon at a quarter before five o'clock."

"Where?"

She named the little café.

"I know it well—used to hang around there," Wilger said.

"That's good! I want you to go to a table far back in the corner and order something to eat, just so you can sit there and not be bothered."

"I getcha!"

"Somebody will come to you—a woman. She will put her left hand over her chest and clear her throat twice—that will be a signal for recognition. Do whatever the woman tells you. Do you understand? No matter how silly it may sound, how unusual you do just as she says—and do not hesitate about it."

"All right!"

"Have you faith in me?"

"I'd bank on you," said Wilger.

"If you have reason to doubt me, better stop and think first," she said. "No matter what happened, would you betray me?"

"No!"

"Very well. Don't act on impulse. Reason things out. And remember that I am not playing the ordinary game. Sometimes I may seem to use peculiar methods, but I generally get results."

"I'll say you do!" Wilger declared, grinning.

"Carry out my orders, then. Do not make the slightest mistake. Just have faith, Wilger—have faith, no matter what happens."

"What can happen?"

"A pinch is always possible. What would you do in case of a pinch, Wilger?"

"Sit tight—like you said."

"Very well. That is all!"

Mme. Madcap ate luncheon at the usual hour and then went to her room. The professor left the house, and so did "Red" Riley. Slade had received orders to remain inside, as he might be needed.

Mme. Madcap called her housekeeper and maid to her room. They had kept rather in the background in the establishment, simply attending to duties, keeping the place reasonably clean, cooking and serving meals. None of the gang knew their relations to Mme. Madcap; but they were women she could trust.

"Your work is done!" she told them. "Here is two hundred dollars each. Slip out of the house some time this afternoon— and forget all about this affair. I know where to find you, if I need you again."

She paid them, and they went away. And then Mme. Madcap went to the closet in the corner of the room and took out a costume. She dressed quickly.

At half past four o'clock, the little door at the end of the narrow passage was opened cautiously, and Mme. Madcap, without her mask and dressed in the uniform of a Salvation Army lassie, walked briskly down the alley.

She walked down the street, alert, going toward the little café she had named to Brute Wilger, and also to the captain of detectives. It was a quarter of five when she reached the corner nearest it, and so she walked on, stopping now and then to look into a shop window, her tambourine tucked beneath her right arm.

Presently she turned back, came to the café again, and glanced through one of the windows. It was a dirty little café with a bar along one side and tables scattered throughout the rest of the room. Rough patrons were in it, and waiters were kept busy.

She passed through the swinging doors. Brute Wilger, she saw, had obeyed instructions. He was sitting at a greasy table far back in a corner, eating slowly. And she saw the captain of detectives, too, at another table not far from Wilger. Evidently he had been unobserved by any who knew him. He had his faced turned away from Wilger, but Mme. Madcap knew that he was watching.

She went to the front of the bar and tendered her tambourine, and received a dime. She long before had decided to double any money she thus collected under false pretenses and send it to the Army. And so she passed on down the bar, offering her tambourine, smiling at the men who gave and at those who did not give impartially.

She finished with those at the bar, and turned toward the tables. Slowly she made her way toward the back of the room. She even stopped before the captain of detectives, and received a dime. And then she approached Brute Wilger.

She stopped before him. She put her left hand to her breast, and cleared her throat twice. Wilger's eyes narrowed.

"Something for the Army, sir?" she asked. And whispering, she added. "Grab the coins out of the tambourine, quick!"

She disguised her voice as she spoke. Wilger flashed her a look, and noticed that she was standing so as to shield him from the others in the café. His hand went up, the tambourine titled, he grasped the handful of coins.

Instantly Mme. Madcap sprang back from the table. Her scream rang out above the din of the room—a woman's scream in such a place! Men whirled toward her.

"He stole! He took my money—"

Brute Wilger, bewildered, was upon his feet now,

bending over the table. Men were rushing toward them, the captain of detectives in the lead.

"He stole the charity money! He took it from the tambourine! See—he has it in his hand!"

Wilger's appearance was against him. His face was flushed, there was a wild look in his eyes, his hands were clenched, his attitude was that of a belligerent.

"What the—" he began.

And then they were upon him, men who did not hesitate to shriek their opinion of a man who would steal charity money from a Salvation Army lassie. They hurled themselves at him, clawing at him, striking at him, and Brute Wilger, frightened, unable to solve this puzzle instantly, tried to fight his way to the wall, tried to fight for the rear door, attempted to escape.

That damned him. They threw him back into the room, while Mme. Madcap crouched beside the table. The captain of detectives battled his way to Wilger's side.

"Under arrest!" he shrieked above the din. "Back, there! Be quiet!"

The confusion ceased. Hard-breathing, angry men ringed around Wilger and the captain and Mme. Madcap.

"What's all this?" the captain demanded. "Stealing from the Salvation Army, Wilger? That's almost the lowest a man can fall! You'll get ten years for this!"

The army woman touched him on the shoulder.

"Perhaps he was not himself," she said. "It is our mission to forgive—"

"But we cannot overlook this, my girl," the captain said. "Such a man must answer to the law."

"I—I do not care to prosecute, if he'll give the money back," she said. "I would not want to testify—"

"We got plenty of witnesses!" the captain said. "I want your names, men—the names of any who saw this and who will help send this cur where he belongs!"

Wilger could not solve this. The woman had given him the prearranged signal, and had told him to take the money. Had he been betrayed? And then he recalled the words of Mme. Madcap—that she worked in peculiar ways, and that he was to have faith in her and "sit tight." Wilger decided in that instant that he would "sit tight" at least for a few days. Perhaps this was an affair that was beyond his reasoning.

Mme. Madcap saw the expression in his face change, and knew the workings of his mind. It was exactly what she had expected Brute Wilger to do—and a day or two would be more than enough.

"I—I am not feeling well," she told the captain. "May I go now, please?"

"Just give me your name and address."

She gave them—fictitious ones, of course, and was allowed to go from the café and up the street.

Two blocks from the café, Mme. Madcap began smiling. Brute Wilger, she knew, would be convicted and given a long term, even without her presence. The police would see to that, since he had been a member of the old Duncan gang. They had other witnesses in plenty, and Wilger had a past record, too.

XV

The Getaway

Safe at home, her costume changed, and her mask on again, Mme. Madcap went to the parlor, where the professor was reading. Sambo appeared in the doorway long enough to report that Hamilton Brone was safe in his cell, and that "Shifty" Slade was slumbering in the lounging-room. "Red" Riley was out.

"And now let us get to business," Mme. Madcap said to the professor, when Sambo had withdrawn. "Our band is rapidly growing smaller, and I must make use of you. Will you carry out my instruction faithfully?"

"Certainly, Mme. Madcap."

"Then I want you, first of all—"

There was a sudden commotion in the hall, and the voices of Sambo and "Red" Riley could be heard in argument. Somebody knocked loudly at the door.

At a sign from Mme. Madcap, the professor crossed the room, unlocked the door and threw it open. "Red" Riley burst in, past Sambo, who would have restrained him.

"They've got Wilger!" Riley exclaimed. "The bulls have got the Brute!"

"What's that?" roared a voice at the door.

"Shifty" Slade had heard the commotion and a part of Riley's words. Now he stormed into the room, fists on hips, under jaw shot out, eyes flaming.

"Then it was a plant!" Slade declared. "They got Marget, too, didn't they? It smells!"

He advanced toward "Red" Riley, his chest heaving.

"I think I'm beginnin' to understand this!" he said. "Chippin' away at my gang, are you, Riley? Tryin' to hand 'em over, are you? You dirty stool-pigeon!"

"Wait! Wait!" Mme. Madcap cried. "Slade, wait! Riley, go back to the wall! This must stop," she commanded. "Do you want to wreck everything? Have you thought of me?"

"Red" Riley, snarling at his foe, walked around the table, picked up his cap and hurried to the door.

"Now!" Mme. Madcap cried. "And you and Slade stay away from each other until I find out the truth!"

Riley snarled again and hurried into the hall and toward the front door. Mme. Madcap faced Slade.

"You're not to fight with Riley until we know!" she said. "I want you to get away from here, too. Go some place where I can reach you by telephone and stay there until midnight. I may want you at any time. Where'll you be?"

"At the headquarters of my gang," Slade said. "I can take care of myself there. There's a phone."

"Give me the number."

Slade did, and Mme. Madcap wrote it on a bit of paper.

Slade left the house, and Sambo retired to the hall. Mme. Madcap sank into her chair at the head of the table.

"You were speaking of—er—work to do when we suffered the interruption," the professor reminded her.

"Yes. I have a package of papers here. They are addressed to a certain police official."

She looked up, and her eyes met those of the professor squarely.

"I am going to slip another paper into the envelope and seal it, and I want you to have it delivered," she said. "Can you trust me?"

"If it is your wish," the professor said.

She wrote rapidly on a piece of paper, thrust it into the envelope, sealed it.

"Go down the street a few blocks and call a messenger," she directed. "Pay him well, and urge him to deliver the package as quickly as possible. Make him think that you are an officer, and that it will cause him trouble if he does not obey."

The professor glanced at the envelope. It was addressed to the captain of detectives. Once more his eyes met those of Mme. Madcap, and then he reached for his hat.

"Return to me as soon as you have done this," she said. "I shall be waiting and on your way out send Sambo in to me."

"It is about done, Sambo," she said when he appeared. "I'll not nee you any more at present."

"I'm ready if you do, miss."

"I know that, Sambo. You, at least, are loyal. But the little game is about over. You will leave the house at once and go about your business. You may have that limousine for your very own. I shall want you in my service, of course, but perhaps you can make some extra money by engaging a man to drive the limousine for you. I may need it again, some time."

"Yes, miss," Sambo said.

"Get a room somewhere and let me know the address in a day or two. If you are caused any trouble, I'll come to your rescue, of course. And here is some money for your immediate needs."

She went on to the parlor, and Sambo, the faithful, went to his own room to pack and leave the hose to carry out her instructions.

Mme. Madcap sat at the end of the long table and waited. And after a time the professor returned.

"The letter is on its way to the proper person," he announced. "Are there any further orders, Mme. Madcap?"

"I want you to pack your things and leave here as soon as possible," she said. "Go to some obscure hotel and register under an assumed name. Keep close to your room tonight and tomorrow morning. Shortly after noon tomorrow, telephone me at this number."

She gave him a little card with a number written upon it.

"It is a private number," she said. "I am trusting you too, you see."

"I am gratified," the professor said. "I shall carry out your orders faithfully. And I shall count the minutes until you allow me to see you again."

He bowed before her and stalked from the room.

Mme. Madcap remained sitting at the table for a short time, until she was sure that the professor was gone, and then she went to a desk in the corner and took a telephone from its place of concealment.

It took her some time to do as she intended, for she was trying to call Lionel Waldron. His valet gave her a number, and the man who answered gave her another, and finally she heard his voice in reply over the wire.

"Mr. Waldron?" she asked.

"Yes."

"This is Mme. Madcap!"

She could hear his gasp over the wire and knew that he was fighting to control himself.

"And to what am I indebted for the pleasure of this call?" he asked.

"Kindly put all sarcasm aside," she said. "You'll probably be glad of this call. I understand that you are hunting Hamilton Brone. Well, my dear Mr. Waldron, you may have him. I am through with him—he is no further use to me."

"What do you mean?" Waldron gasped.

"Exactly what I say. Oh, he is still alive, if that is what is troubling you. And I am going to tell you where you may find him—on certain conditions."

"What are the conditions?" Waldron asked.

"You are to go for him alone, or with some of your private detectives. But I suppose you'll want to do that. You don't want the police to get him first, do you? And when you find him, if you look around—well you will find evidence enough to clear him of the silly charge of having helped me rob the Darcan residence. The police may be called in, then, of course, so they will cease annoying Hamilton Brone. The other condition is this—that you be in your rooms at noon tomorrow, to receive a telephone call."

"I promise to fulfill those two conditions," Waldron said.

"Very well. I know that you are a gentleman and can be trusted. You will find Hamilton Brone in a room on the third floor of a house the address of which I shall soon give you. You may take your men and go after him as soon as you like."

Mme. Madcap hesitated a moment, and then spoke the number of the house. An instant later, she hung up the receiver, dashed down the stairs, and entered the little passage. She hurried to the end, removed her mask and hung it up, put on her hat, and stepped out into the alley. Then she went on to the street and hastened toward the nearest subway station.

XVI

Brone is Found

Waldron was by no means a coward, and so he called to him only one operative noted for courage and presence of mind in emergencies, explaining the affair to him, and went with him to the address Mme. Madcap had given.

They went to the third floor. They came to the prison room and found the door locked. Listening at the keyhole, Waldron could hear a man moaning.

He hurled himself against the door, but failed to break it in. Then he resorted to skeleton keys, found one that would serve, and threw the door open. Weapons held ready, Waldron and his companion darted into the room, found the light switch, snapped it.

They gasped at what they saw. There were the two cells, one empty, one containing Hamilton Brone. He gave a shriek of delight when he saw

Waldron, clutched at the bars and tried to shake them.

"Here's bunch of keys on the couch!" the operative called.

He tossed them to Waldron, who fitted one into the lock of the cell door. Hamilton Brone sprang out, weeping hysterically, trying to laugh, trying to talk and merely babbling meaninglessly. Waldron aided him to the couch.

He ordered Brone to remove the convict's suit and dress in his own clothing.

"Talk," he said. "It'll soothe your nerves. Brace up, Hamilton! You're about ready to go to pieces."

"I—she drugged me in the limousine that night I left the café with her," Brone said. "Next thing I knew, I awoke in that cell, dressed like a convict. A man came in dressed like a guard. He—he told me that I had murdered Melkington, that I had been sentenced for life. He convinced me, finally. I couldn't remember anything. He said I was in this room because I had raised such a disturbance."

When Brone had finished his story, Waldron told of the attempt to implicate him in the Darcan robbery and mark him as a member of Mme. Madcap's band of criminals. Then he finished by telling of the telephone message which had led to his liberation.

"Now hurry and finish dressing," he ordered. "We must get out of here. The police may come, and I want to know how to clear you before we meet them. Get into your coat." He turned to the operative. "Go down and get a taxi and have it at the end of the alley," he directed. "Have the curtains drawn in it."

The operative hurried away. Lionel Waldron assisted Brone to the door, snapped out the lights, aided the semi-hysterical man down the hall and the stairs. He darted into the parlor for a moment, to see whether there was any evidence he desired. And he saw what he had not before—a note addressed to himself.

Waldron picked it up, tore it open, and read it swiftly.

> Mr. Waldron—It is not remorse that makes me do this, but the knowledge that I have done enough and that I am making an innocent woman suffer. Hamilton Brone has been my prisoner, and nothing more. He has been held in that cell upstairs since the evening he left the café with me. Those fingerprints on the safe were put there by me. I transferred them from a cake of soap Hamilton Brone had used to a fine rubber glove coated with a sensitive chemical mixture. You will find the glove in the drawer of the table; keep it and prove Hamilton Brone's innocence of the charge of burglary. I wrote the note to the police about the fingerprints. Possibly I shall tell you more later.
> MME. MADCAP

Waldron darted to the table, drew out the drawer, found the glove, wrapped it carefully in newspaper, and put it into his pocket. Then he grasped Brone by the arm and hurried to the lower floor and the entrance of the house.

XVII

The Empty Nest

"Shifty" Slade, sitting at a table in the rear room of the greasy little resort where his gang formerly had made its headquarters, waiting impatiently for the message from Mme. Madcap, looking toward the front of the resort each time the telephone rang. And then he saw a detective of his acquaintance enter by the front door, look around the room, and step to the case to purchase a cigar.

Slade thought nothing of that. The officer was one who continually was assigned to the district. He made a practice of dropping in at the different resorts patronized by gangsters. But Slade watched him—watched him so closely that he did not notice the rear door open and two other detectives step inside quietly and approach his table, did not know they were near until one of them spoke.

"We want you, Slade!"

"It's a little matter of murder, Slade. We've got you dead to rights—evidence enough to convict a regiment. It happened a year ago, Slade—a well-known young man about town got his head cracked, and you cracked it."

Slade's face paled; his jaw dropped.

"Dead to rights!" the detective said. "Somebody was kind enough to send us all the evidence by messenger. It took us about an hour to find out that the stuff was good. We've got you, Slade! And there is another thing, too—a little matter of a safe deposit box belonging to a well-known actress—"

"So that's it!" he cried. "Double-crossed, am I? That she-devil of a Mme. Madcap!"

"You grow interesting," one of the detectives remarked, grinning.

"I can be interestin', all right. She's thrown me down, and I'll throw her down. Wear a mask, will she? You want Mme. Madcap? I'll tell you where you can get her! I've been workin' with her—understand? Tip me off to the bulls, will she?"

"Just talk," one of them suggested.

"Talk, is it? I can give you the address. She's probably there now. You'll find a lot of interestin' things—some more of the gang, and that guy Hamilton Brone locked in a cell on the third floor, kept prisoner. I can tell you all about Mme. Madcap. Wear a mask, will she? Maybe you've got the nerve to tear it off!"

A sudden thought came to "Shifty" Slade then. The expression of his face changed. Marget, Wilger, himself—all were members of the old Duncan gang.

And nobody knew better than "Shifty" Slade what had happened inside that gang.

He gulped, went limp, and one of the detectives grasped him by the arm. Slade knew that he was done—it was only a question of time. And the bitter thirst for vengeance came to him again.

He spoke it, in a low voice. Handcuffs snapped on his wrists. One of the men took him away, and the other hurried to the nearest telephone booth.

Fifteen minutes later, a police department automobile disgorged its load of officers in front of Mme. Madcap's house, and the officers hurried to the front door, the detective who had taken Slade into custody leading them.

"Slade was right!" he said after scouring the house. "But we're too late. The nest is empty!"

XVIII

"No Matter!"

At noon the following day, Lionel Waldron received the telephone call he had anticipated.

"If you wish to learn all about Mme. Madcap," said a woman's voice, "please come to the residence of Miss Dorcas Darcan just as soon as possible, and bring Hamilton Brone with you."

The butler opened the door at Waldron's ring and ushered the two men inside.

Dorcas Darcan came into the room and stopped just inside the door to look them over.

"Did you know of a prominent criminal know as William Duncan?"

"Yes; heard of the famous, or infamous Duncan gang," Waldron replied. "He was sentenced a few months ago to serve twenty-five years for burglary."

"It was my house he was robbing when he was caught!" Hamilton Brone exclaimed.

"Exactly," said Dorcas Darcan. "I shall tell you this first— the woman you have known as Mme. Madcap is the daughter of the man you knew as William Duncan. And now for the story.

"William Duncan was a peculiar man in many ways. He craved adventure and excitement, and after the death of his wife he gratified his desire by turning criminal and becoming a shrewd one. He left his mark behind him often, but never was caught, and he had a band of men who were experts in their line. He ruled them with a strict discipline, made them obey orders implicitly.

"Duncan was not a criminal for gain; he gave most of the profits to his men. He also was known by another name, and he had money that he had acquired honestly. This he invested and multiplied. He had a daughter, you see, and wanted to leave her well provided for. He had her educated abroad and, then she returned and learned of her father's double life.

"She adored her father, and the lure of the underworld interested her. She knew that all his interest in life, outside her, was in his nefarious work, and so she did not attempt to dissuade him. He used to tell her of his accomplishments; this girl knew as much of the underworld as its denizens, yet she was aloof from it, not touched by its sordidness. And she worshiped her father.

"And then her father was taken in the act of robbery. The evidence was conclusive, and he was sentenced to twenty-five years in prison. He was fifty years old when he was sentenced, so it is probably that he will never come out alive.

"His daughter was heartbroken, of course. Nobody knew that she was the daughter of William Duncan, for she was known by her right name, and it was not Duncan. Before her father was taken to prison to begin his long sentence, he had all his property turned over to her. She is a rich woman.

"And he told her something else—how he had been betrayed by the members of his own gang. One of them was ambitious to assume the leadership, and he influenced the others. The robbery of Mr. Brone's house had been planned, and one of the gang telephoned the details to the police. William Duncan was captured, and all the others escaped. He went to trail, to prison, without betraying them. But he had ascertained that they had betrayed him.

"His daughter learned it from his own lips and swore vengeance. She has ample funds. She purchased that house downtown that you now know as the headquarters of Mme. Madcap. She posed as a criminal and managed to get with her the three old members of the Duncan gang, the men who had betrayed her father.

"Do you begin to understand now? 'Shifty' Slade was the man who arranged the betrayal. 'Gentleman Joe' Marget and Brute Wilger were those who aided him. One by one, Mme. Madcap betrayed them into the hands of the police, as they had her father. She had her vengeance. And that is her story."

"And are you Mme. Madcap?" Waldron asked.

"Oh, no! One moment, please!"

She stepped to the portieres that separated the room from another, and opened them. Into the room came the professor, a masked woman on his arm.

"This is Mme. Madcap," Dorcas Darcan said.

A light laugh came from behind the mask, and then it was torn away. And Lionel Waldron and Hamilton Brone gasped their surprise. Side by side they stood, Dorcas Darcan and Mme. Madcap, twins to the last eyelash, twins in appearances, in voice, in manner.

"Do you understand now?" Dorcas asked. "The story I told you is true, except that there were two daughters—twins. William Duncan's correct name was Darcan. I am Dorcas— this is Doris."

Hamilton Brone sprang to his feet.

"But what had I to do with it?" he cried. "Why persecute me for what some criminals did?"

Doris motioned for him to sit down again, and sat down herself, still holding the mask in her hand.

"My father was captured in your residence, Mr. Brone," she said. "Do you remember the night of the robbery? The captain of detectives who had been given the tip passed it on to you, and together you waited for my father to walk into the trap. And, in court, a point was made of whether my father had a weapon in his possession. It was a small matter to you. Without thinking, you said that he had a re- volver, and had thrown it through the window dur- ing the struggle. Do you know what it meant to my father? It meant the difference between ten years and twenty-five of his life in a perpetual hell! It meant that, instead of coming out a broken man in a few years, he probably would not come out at all.

"You, thoughtless Hamilton Brone, eager to have done with your testimony and be gone to meet some woman, condemned my father to a double sentence. My father was a criminal, the way the world looks at it, and I have nothing to say because he is punished. But those extra fifteen years he does not deserve.

"Do you see why I punished you, Hamilton Brone? I made you a laughing-stock, then I forced the town to believe that you were a criminal. Had I not felt sorry for your wife, I should have gone through with it. As it is, you are punished sufficiently; it will take you a lifetime to live down.

"I drugged you and had you placed in that cell. You remember your feelings, I am sure. And remember, please, that because of your false, hurried testimony, my father will have twenty-five years of that, instead of ten."

"What of the rest of the gang?" asked Waldron.

"I got Slade and Wilger and Marget in my gang and betrayed them one at a time. "Red" Riley did not know; the professor, here, did not know. I staged a robbery here, in my own house, so that those men would have confidence in me and follow my orders blindly—orders that would lead them into the hands of the police. It cost me only a few hundred dollars, and I have plenty of money. I merely retained the pearls and articles of value of course. There is no penalty—a person cannot rob her own house!"

"How about the abduction of Hamilton Brone?" Waldron asked.

"Do you wish to press the charge?" she asked

Brone pleasantly. "When I walked out of that house downtown, Mme. Madcap ceased to exist. It is true that I own the house, true also that a friend of mine rented it from me though an agent. I could say I did not know the tenants. Do you think you could force a jury to believe that one of the Darcan sisters, who are wealthy, would stoop to being Mme. Madcap? And you cannot find proof that William Darcan and William Duncan were the same man.

"I think it would be best, Mr. Waldron, to drop the affair right here and let the police think what they will. I understand that they are searching for Prof. Salwick, but his alibi is prepared. Mme. Madcap they simply will be unable to find. As for Mr. Brone, who was suspected of being a member of Mme. Madcap's band, I already have showed you how to clear him. It will have to be a mystery, of course, why he was abducted. There will be a certain amount of suspicion—but that will be his punishment. Perhaps it will be a lesson, too. I understand he has a charming wife who loves him. He may thank her that I did not ruin him utterly, then turn him over as I did the others, with evidence that could not be broken down.

"I am glad that it is over—glad that I have avenged my father. It was terrible to lie and deceive, but I feel that I was justified. They lied and betrayed. They broke the unwritten law of the underworld, and I broke it to punish them. Well, what is the verdict, Mr. Waldron? Do you drop this affair and forget Mme. Madcap? Or do you wish to fight? I assure you that I am fully prepared."

Waldron opened his mouth to reply, but Hamilton Brone was ahead of him.

"We drop it!" Brone said.

"Professor," she said, softly, "for a man of brains, you are slow to understand."

At that moment, the professor understood.

"It is a glorious world," he announced, his arms around her. "Mme. Madcap, eh? We must forget that name and use something more intimate. Dorcas? Or was it Doris? No matter!"

THE END